The Shed

M. C Ronen

To Sarah and
        Christopher,
with great appreciation
and respect for your
work.   Maya xx

* A word of caution: some parts of
this book might be triggering.

ISBN-13: 978-1-7200-8438-9

To my beloved Denni and Melli,

children of the revolution.

Keep standing up for what is right, even if you stand alone.

You are not alone

CONTENTS

ACKNOWLEDGMENTS

I wish to thank my good friend Emma B for helping me with first readings and editing early drafts. Emma, your advice was always sound and on point. But mostly I thank you for believing in me and in this book, and for your encouragement along the way. To my mum and dad, thank you for your love and support. Thank you to my husband, son and daughter, for making my life complete. We make such a great team. My son was also my first reader, even though he was under the target readership age (as he had just turned 13 at the time). My love, you gave me some good criticism and some fantastic plot ideas, and I have used them all. To Phoebe, for your total love and devotion. To Carlos and Hermione, for your endless cuteness. To Luther, who is running in the golden fields beyond the rainbow bridge, you are always in my heart my sweet boy.
Last but not least, I wish to thank, from the bottom of my heart, the countless passionate, wonderful people around the world, who spend time and energy fighting speciesism and oppression, carrying the vegan revolution on their shoulders, bringing us a better future and freedom for all. You are all heroes.

AUTHOR'S NOTE

While this book contains some scenes of violence carried out by the oppressed against their oppressors, these are for artistic purposes. The author does not support a violent struggle.

1 THE RAID

There are those days when, as soon as you open your eyes, you just know they are going to be different. Something in the air tastes different in your mouth. The sky weighs heavily on your mind, the wind blows your hair differently, maybe less knowingly. I don't know what it is. It just feels like something is about to happen, like your soul is telling you to look out, to be more watchful or something. I still haven't figured it out. Some people used to say that it was a gift I had. "She can smell danger a mile away," they used to say. I heard them. They never said it judgingly or with bad intentions. Actually, the way they used to say it, it sounded almost like a compliment.

The first time I heard them say that about me, I was a little younger. It was after the raid on the farm. Some people came during the night thinking they had a right to just take whatever they wanted, just grab and take. I was just over thirteen seasons old.

I woke up in the middle of the night. It was very dark, but I had this feeling, this heaviness in the pit of my stomach, the metallic taste of dread in my mouth. Something just wasn't right. I could feel it in the air.

The night at the farm was always rather quiet. I used to love listening to it. The wind was very kind, it blew through the wheat fields and the corn fields very gently, always making a soft *whoosh* sound as it passed. I could have listened to it for hours. And there was also the sound of the crickets, singing to each other, serenading into the night. I enjoyed their singing. A cricket once got stuck in my room somehow and I knew, just by the way it was singing, that it wasn't happy about it. I took it out, just outside the door, and he disappeared into the night. I felt rather lonely after that, in my quiet room. I thought maybe next time a cricket gets stuck in my room I'll keep it. But it didn't happen again. On the night of the raid the strangest thing was, that there was no singing. I couldn't hear any crickets, and I couldn't hear the whoosh of the wind on the fields. There was only a weird far away sound, like a rolling thunder. And the little stones I kept near my bed for when I played Jacks with my friends were sort of shaking ever so slightly. Something inside me was screaming at me to get up. I went to the bedroom window. The window in my bedroom was small, overlooking the glorious orchard my mom always claimed she planted half herself, and beyond it just fields that rolled on and on past the farm and forever into the horizon. There was a gravel road that stretched to the east of the orchard and cut through the fields like a white scar. If I stretched my neck far out the window and looked to the right, I could just glimpse the edge of the gate to the farm - a big, heavy, iron gate that was mostly locked. On the night of the raid I could just make out small lights far down on the road ahead. I knew this was not a good sign. Lights on the road in the middle of the night could not be a good sign.

I really don't remember much of that night to be honest. Flashes of memory are all that I can recall. I was acting mostly out of some sub conscious auto drive. It can happen to me sometimes, when things happen and I need to act quickly, to make decisions quickly. I just act, I just make decisions. I remember that I ran out of my room and down the stairs. I was still in my night gown and barefoot, I was screaming "Lights! Lights! Lights on the road!" It woke almost everyone up. I remember running out of the room and out of the building and into where my mom was sleeping. I nearly busted the door. I made such a ruckus, I was certain that everyone heard me. But it wasn't so. Not everyone woke. If they had, they would not have been taken.

Mom looked into my eyes. That's all she did – just looked deeply into my eyes. My mom had the most beautiful dark blue eyes that when she looked at you with *that* certain look of hers, you felt her gaze piercing you through the eyes and into the depth of your soul. I don't know what she found at the depth of my soul, but she just nodded.

"Take the baby," she said to me with this unfamiliar tremor in her voice. She never had a tremor in her voice before, ever, and that truly shook me. "Run to the fields – to the pond."

All I can remember from that night is that I ran back to the babies' room and grabbed my sister Antim, from her crib. I held her in my arms and I just ran. I ran into the dark of night breathing heavy, whispering to Antim to stay calm. I ran and I ran, while dark thoughts kept pestering me. I was agonising with guilt for not making sure my friend Rosichi was running with me. Why didn't I take Rosichi? I always took care of her, especially since her mother disappeared. But I kept running all the same. I could hear my mother yelling some things to the other women. I heard screeches. I remember looking back, seeing the lights pulling up close to the gate, but I kept running. There were other feet running behind me and I could hear the echoes of heavy breaths. The sound of a huge, terrifying explosion by the gate rolled through the farm like magnified thunder. It made us all jump and scream as we ran. But from that moment I don't remember much else except running.

The farm was huge. I used to think it went on and on forever. I *knew* that it had an end somewhere, and that there was a world outside of the farm, but it was so vast that it was just as easy to believe there was nothing else. Only the farm. I never saw the other side of the fence but I knew it was there. It must have been, just the same threatening tall fence that surrounded our living quarters, the massively built fence that had a big and heavy gate that I could see the edge of, if I stretched my head out of the window. The gate that had just then been exploded by the raiders. No one was allowed to touch that fence under any circumstances. It was one of the first lessons we were taught on the farm. Don't touch the fence. Ever. I assumed the fence had to go all around the farm, but that night, even though I ran and ran, I still did not get to the other side.

There was a tiny muddy pond far into the corn field. It was nothing more than a puddle really. I used to go there sometimes by myself, but the first time I had seen the pond was with my mom. She took me there once to show it to me. It was one of those rare days she spent with me back then, when she was almost happy. That's where I was running to.

It was dark. I was not alone by then. I could hear the other girls and some of the women. Everyone knew the pond, although it was rare for anyone else except me to go there. I laid down on the ground, cradling Antim gently in my arms, rocking her tenderly. She was such a beautiful baby, with Mom's deep blue eyes, a shock of blond hair, wearing her little beanie hat. She was cooing a bit so I covered her pink cheeks with little kisses. "Hey little Antim," I said as I laid her carefully by my side. I remember feeling heavy. Mom said I fainted.

The next thing I remember was being on the ground, my head on my mother's lap as she was stroking my hair. She loved stroking my hair. My hair is long and thick and sort of copper-brown. She loved patting it.

"You did all right Sunny," she was whispering to me.

Sunny. That's my name.

On the farm, you normally had two names, the name your mother gave you, and the name you were given by the community or your friends, which is usually the name you got stuck with. My name was always just Sunny. Mom used to say that the day I was born was rather grey and cloudy, but when I came out into the world, almost immediately I opened my eyes, as if I was in a great hurry to see it all. I had a look that was full of excitement and eagerness. She decided I was displaying the early signs of a sunny personality. I never quite comprehended the meaning of a 'sunny personality', I don't even think that it proved to be necessarily true about me. In any case, the name was never replaced with another. No one ever dared give me a nickname. Maybe they were afraid to defy my mom. She had some serious standing in the farm community.

"Well done Sunny," some of other women said. They were saying it gently. Sincerely. "Thank Mercy you could smell danger a mile away."

I sat up. My body was stiff. It was first light. We were all gathered in the corn field by the muddy pond.

I rubbed off the numbness in my arm. "What happened Mom?" I asked, my voice tired and croaky.

"There was a raid on the farm" Mom said. She put her hand softly on my face. She looked severe and tired but her hand was warm and soft.

"What's a raid?" I asked, still confused.

"It's when people come to the farm thinking they can take whatever they like!" an angry voice responded. It was Freckles, who was pacing back and forth by the murky water. She was about the same age as my mom, maybe slightly younger. I never even knew her real name, we have always known her as Freckles, a name she must have earned years before, and not without a very good reason.

I turned my eyes back to my mom. "I don't understand".

Mom gave me one of her little smiles. "There are people outside the farm that must think they can come here and take us," she said. Her voice was soft and steady. She did not sound at all alarmed or scared. I was glad that the tremor was gone. It was reassuring.

"Did they take someone?" I asked. I looked around. I couldn't see Rosichi. "Where is Rosichi?" I asked with real urgency.

Mom smiled, "She is ok Sunny. She is sleeping right over there". She pointed with her face over the other side of the pond. Rosichi was there, nestled on the ground with other girls. They were sleeping. I was so relieved.

"You are a good girl, Sunny," Mom said. Her eyes were kind.

"Did they take anyone?" I asked again.

Mom sighed.

It turned out that the people who raided the farm took four women, four babies, and three girls. One of the girls was a close friend of mine. Her name was Pearl. She was always such a happy one. Her giggles were catching, you were compelled to join. Her smile was so wide, glorious and disarming, that no one stood a chance sulking for long. She had a mesmerizingly beautiful dark skin and large brown eyes you could just sink into. Everyone loved her.

Pearl was gone.

"Where? Where did they take them Mom?" I asked.

Mom was quiet.

"Mom?"

She just looked at my sister Antim. Rocking her gently.

"Mom?"

"Enough with the questions, Sunny" Freckles said rather angrily. "They are gone. Gone. What else is there to know?"

I looked at my mom, begging. I could feel big warm salty tears forming in my eyes, getting fuller and heavier, ready to sneak out of my eyes any minute.

"Mom?" I whispered.

Mom's eyes were kind. "I don't know Sunny" she said. "I don't know"....

I let the tears roll. I cried all the way back to the dorms.

The White Suits came that same morning and fixed the gate. It looked even heavier now.

There were no more raids after that one.

2 THE DAY AFTER THE RAID

Mom came to see me just outside the girls' dorms the day after the raid. It wasn't often that Mom came to the girls' dorms to see me. I thought she wanted to check on me after the raid, because Pearl was taken and she was worried for me. Everyone on the farm was still quite shaken.

It was a nice day and we sat outside by the dorms' entrance, observing absentmindedly the men who were repairing the gate. Some we had seen before and some were new, men with orange overalls and funny looking helmets. The gate was destroyed in the explosion and had to be completely reassembled.

Mom sat me near the small thorny bush. The thorny bush was a bit useless, it gave no shade, it had no flowers, it had no smell, but it gave us a little bit of privacy. There were makeshift benches by the bush, they were ancient, I remember them there as a toddler. We sat together. Mom put her arm around me. I leaned my head against her shoulder. I loved the feeling of comfort Mom always gave me.

"How are you doing this morning, Sunny?" she asked me, in a very soft voice. She could be so caring, my mom, so soft and gentle… I don't know why, but just her voice alone brought tears to my eyes.

"I'm OK," I answered. I don't know if I really was OK. Probably I wasn't OK. But I couldn't think of something comprehensive to say.

We sat there for a while. Watching the men fussing around the fence. The fence was so formidable and massive, it was almost like a complete other *being*, constantly living with us, framing our world. Like a beast of deadly powers, it had a thick skeleton, separated by heavy poles every few meters, like vertebrae. The top of the fence was bended, pointing inwards. The inwards pointing part was stretched nearly flat. As a child I remember fantasizing about climbing the fence and standing on top of it, bouncing on the stretched part. Of course, I never did. It wasn't just the fact that it was utterly forbidden to even come close to the fence, I was actually afraid of it. The fence was alive. I knew, because every time I even vaguely considered trying to climb it, it gave the most terrifying hiss a beast could utter.

One of the orange suited men turned and looked at us. He had a short fair hair, slim build. I could have been wrong but for a moment there I thought he was smiling at us.

"He's a good-looking chap, don't you think?" Mom said out of the blue.

"I don't know. Maybe," I replied.

I really didn't know. What makes a man good-looking? I was not used to looking at men. We had no boys in the farm. No men. What did they even look like? I'm sure some were nice and others were not. Some were pleasant to look at while others were not, but I had absolutely no idea what constituted a good-looking man. No idea whatsoever.

"*I* think he is good looking," Mom said.

"Mom!" I was a bit surprised by where the conversation was going. Mom never raised topics like that with me. We did not talk about anything much, to be honest. When I needed to start wearing a bra because my breasts grew heavy, Mom just came over one day and said "You have breasts now Sunny". And she took me to her dorms and fitted me with one. It was slightly too big and rather uncomfortable, but that was it. No fussing around.

Mom followed the good-looking man with her eyes. I was getting a little embarrassed by her noticeable interest.

"Mom, will you stop watching him?" I asked, trying to hide my face in her shoulder.

"What do you reckon they are doing?" Mom asked, her eyes still on the good-looking man.

"They are fixing the gate," I said. Wasn't it obvious?

"Why are they using the rug?" Mom was wondering aloud.

I raised my head and I noticed they were using a big, heavy rug to cover part of the fence. The rug was blue and massive. It covered both sides of the fence completely, stretched on top of the flat part like a little bench. I didn't pay much attention to it before. Maybe only I was observing them absentmindedly. Mom was surely paying them a lot of attention. Especially the good-looking man.

"It's probably because the fence can kill you if you touch it," I said. "Maybe it is some sort of a shield."

We grew up with the absolute knowledge that you must never, ever do that or your brains will fry.

"Clever girl," Mom said and fluffed my hair.

We sat there quietly for a while longer. Mom kept following the good-looking man with her eyes. Every now and then he turned to look at her. Mom was a very beautiful woman. Everyone said so. They used to say that this must have been the reason she was still going. I'm not sure I knew what they meant by that; I don't know where she was going. She was always just at the farm. She was always just going to The Shed.

The good-looking man nodded to my mom and smiled. Mom smiled back. It was all becoming a bit too embarrassing.

Mom was quiet. She patted my back with her hand. I liked that. Then out of the blue she asked me "Did you start getting your monthly bleeding?"

That's it. I couldn't believe she was talking to me about that stuff.

"Well, have you or not?"

"No. I haven't." None of my friends had their monthly bleeding yet, but we were told by the women at the community room about body functions and the menstrual cycle. It sounded gross. I was not looking forward to it at all.

Then, Mom took my chin in her hands and turned my face towards her face. She stared into my eyes. She had *that* look. "Sunny, promise me that when you get your bleed you will tell me."

"Yeah. OK."

"Promise me. I am serious Sunny. Promise you will tell me. Immediately. Before anyone else you tell ME."

I started to get a little nervous by that whole talk.

"OK Mom. I promise."

Mom fluffed my hair with her hand again. "OK. Run along now." And she sent me on my way.

I don't remember where I went, but I do remember looking back and seeing her walking towards the good-looking man. The way she moved, it was amazing, soft and strong. Her thighs so uncharacteristically swaying from side to side. The man dropped everything he was doing. You could see he was very interested in talking to her. I kept walking. I could hear Mom saying, "Hi… I'm

Stella." The man was answering. I wasn't listening any more. Something in the way Mom said it, "Hi… I'm Stella." I had never, ever heard her use her voice like that. Sugary, sweet, like a warm apple coated in maple syrup.

3 SUMMONED

"Sunny, your mom wants you".

Two seasons had passed since the raid. It was becoming a distant memory in the collective recollection of the farm community. I wasn't thinking of Pearl that often any more.

I was spending the morning in the kale garden watching a large black beetle trying to dig into the ground. Ever since I woke up that morning I had a metallic taste of dread in my mouth, fear of a certain darkness looming settled in the pit of my stomach, just like it did the day the farm was raided.

I often attended to the kale garden. "Be kind to the earth and the earth will return your kindness," Mom taught me. The kale garden was tucked away north of the dorms, growing on the verge of the wheat fields. It was sort of peaceful there as not many girls liked digging out weeds and raking the dry soil.

I looked up. Snotty was there waiting for me to respond. "Your mom wants you," she repeated once she had my attention.

Snotty was a good seven or eight seasons younger than me so she and I never really hung out together. But she was one of the young girls who absolutely loved following the older girls around and tried desperately to fit in, even though most of the time she was completely ignored. It's not that she wasn't likeable, she was, but she was younger, that was all. Being younger was a good enough reason for the older girls not to want to hang out with you. But she was a sweet looking girl. Her eyes were slightly slanted. She had silky brown hair that she always wore loose on her shoulders, a button nose that had only a few freckles spread on it, which was rather cute, I thought. You can imagine why we called her Snotty. I admit, it is not the nicest of names to be calling someone, but when she was a toddler it was the perfect match. Trust me. It probably did not fit her quite as much anymore, but the name stuck.

I took my time. I knew something was coming and I guess I just didn't want it to.

"Sunny!" Snotty was getting restless.

"OK, OK…" I got up from the ground and gave my knees and legs a good rubbing to get the soil off. "Why on earth did my mom send *you*? Where's Rosichi?"

Snotty seemed a little offended. "How should I know?"

Rosichi was my best friend. She was closer to me than even Pearl was before she was taken. We were born on the same season. We spent all our babyhood and our toddlerhood and our childhood together. We were the same age but she was always smaller than me and a little weak looking. Her hair was fair as was her flawless skin, her eyes were bright grey and she was always such an energetic little capsule. Her real name was Rosy Cheeks. That's a full-on name no doubt. As a little girl I couldn't even pronounce it properly so it just came out as Rosichi and the name stuck. Rule of the farm. To be honest, her cheeks were not even that rosy, but I suppose they were when she was born.

Rosichi wasn't keen on the kale garden so she rarely joined me there. But most other times we were together. She was not just my best friend, she was like a sister to me. I felt responsible for her in a way, especially after her mother was gone. That was four seasons ago. Before the raid.

I am a fast walker but this time I was deliberately walking slowly. Snotty had no problem keeping up with me. She tried to take my hand in hers, but her hand felt warm and a bit sweaty so I shook her off. I shouldn't have done that; I am a little embarrassed that I did. It wasn't a nice thing to do, she was only a little girl. She stopped on her tracks. I knew I must have hurt her feelings.

"Sorry Snotty…. It's just that my hands are dirty," I backtracked into a white lie, "from digging in the kale garden… Come on, let's walk together."

She was still considering it when we both heard the Sky Noise.

Every now and then, long before the raid, a Sky Noise appeared. We used to get lots of those appear in the sky on the weeks leading to the raid. The Sky Noise always announced itself with a prolonged humming sound before we could see it. They came out of nowhere and they disappeared far into the horizon. Sure enough, within seconds I could spot the cubic black object in the sky. It just floated up high in the air. The thing hovered over us a few seconds and disappeared.

After the Sky Noise disappeared, Snotty was quick to join me, walking faster by my side.

Mom was waiting for me at the entrance to the women's dorms. You could spot her from afar. She was a beautiful woman, my mom. Her legs were strong and long. She was standing tall and proud. She was one of the eldest in the farm community, but to me she did not seem that old at all. Farm life takes its toll on women. But my mom was still there, untouchable. She stood there looking so graceful, you could almost forget how dreary the place looked.

The women's dorm was a dark wooden building, two stories high. It must have been painted once but the color was all sad and chipped. The windows were small so not much light came into the rooms. It was a dusty and gloomy place and I really didn't like spending much time in there, unless I was spending it with my mom.

I waved to her as I got closer. She waved back but I could just read her nervousness in the way she looked, in the way she moved her hand, in the way her mouth twitched ever so slightly. I ran those last few steps, throwing myself into her arms.

She put her long arms around me and kissed me on the crown of my head. I was rather tall for my age, but my mom was even taller. I was very nearly fifteen seasons old, but I still felt like a kid when I was with her. We did not often have time to spend together, just us. I ached for her company. She was gentle and wise but also strong in a way that was subtle and humbling.

*

One of the most precious memories I have with my mom, is from the day she took me for a surprise walk to the pond.

I was playing Jacks with my friends at the community room which stood at the back, right hand side of the women's dorms. I must have been no more than five seasons old because that's just about when my mother recovered from the death of my sister Precious. It was a horrid time, but she must have felt much stronger and happier on that day. Seeing her appear at the community room, all dressed up and clean, her hair brushed and tied up… I could feel little bubbles of sheer joy pulsing up and down my spine. She just put her finger to her lips signaling that I should be quiet, and took me by the hand. The day was cool but warming up and we just walked and walked in complete silence. Every now and then she looked at me. There was a smile in her blue eyes. Hand in hand we kept walking in silence, well past the wheat fields and into the corn fields until we arrived at a small clearance with a sorry looking pond at its center. On that day, with her by my side, that place seemed downright magical to me.

"This was a glorious place once," she said suddenly. "Many, many seasons ago, there used to be magical creatures living here."

I just looked at her, puzzled. There was nothing in the pond. Just brown water of old rain.

Once, a very long time ago, before the catastrophes struck this planet, there were creatures living here, beautiful animals of all kinds. I saw them in books. Marvelous creatures. They were all mostly wiped out. Only insects and some humans were left. I sometimes wished they all came back. The creatures, I mean, not so much the other humans. I spent quite a lot of time wondering what they sounded like. I imagined a world rich with sound and color. It made me so sad, the loss of so much beauty.

"Here," she put her hands into the pocket of her blouse and took out a few little seedlings. "How about you put these in the ground close to the water and we'll see if something grows."

I dug a tiny trench by the water where the ground was nice and soft and put the seedlings in. A sleepy worm was not happy about the disturbance. "Look Mom!" I said. We watched the worm sliding back deeper into the ground.

"So beautiful," she said, smiling.

We covered the seedlings together.

"What did we just plant, Momma?" I asked once we were standing over the little mound.

"Hope," she answered.

I didn't understand. It took me plenty of visits to the pond to figure it out. They were flowers. Beautiful tulips. They grew all beautiful and colorful and tall. They were stunning to look at. I could stand there for hours just looking at their beauty. In some way they reminded me of my mom. Tall, strong, beautiful, and a little sad.

In the end the weather changed and the tulips died and they never grew back again. That was it for hope, I suppose. Mom never took me to the pond again and we didn't spend much time together any more.

4 MOM'S ORDERS

"Sunny," Mom said, shaking me out of those memories of bygone times and back into the present. She released her arms and pushed me from her body. Her eyes were severe. She had *that* look. The taste of doom returned to my mouth. I could feel the bile in my stomach.

"The White Suits are in the Sick Room," she said.

The Sick Room is what farm folk called the place where the sick and wounded were taken. We did not use terms like 'clinic' or 'hospital'.

I got choked up by that.

"The White Suits are here?"

Mom had no time for questions, "Sunny, listen to me," she said, as she bended a little to put her head closer to my ear. "You and Rosichi must *run*."

I wasn't expecting that. "To the pond?" I asked.

"No. Run! Run far away. Get out of this place!"

There was an unfamiliar desperation in her voice. I almost could not recognize it.

"NOW!" she said and pushed me away from her.

So, I did what I was told.

Rosichi was not in the community room. All the girls of my age were not there, only the younger ones were playing. Snotty and her friends.

I peeked through the sliding doors to the kitchen. That was where I'd usually find Rosichi when I returned from my venture to the kale garden. She loved cooking. We did not have much but there was always plenty of delicious food being cooked in that kitchen. Kale, broccoli, corn, lentils and chickpeas, some snow peas and bell peppers. We had grains to make bread and buns. And we had plenty of apples, mandarins, avocados and mangos from the orchard. Sometimes we had tomatoes when the weather was not causing havoc. I loved the juicy red jewels. It was a real treat. Once a year we received a delivery of dates and raisins, and some dark chocolate for birthday treats.

"Are you looking for Rosichi?" Snotty asked.

"Yes. Did you see her?"

"All the big girls were going to The Shed," she replied.

Now that was bad.

The Shed was normally completely out of bounds. It was a massive red brick building at the west corner of the living compound, but still quite far from the community room and the dorms. There were no windows to The Shed. It had a big, white, creaking gate that was usually locked. Girls were not allowed to get in there, only the grown-up women went. No one talked about what went on in there or what the women were doing. Mom used to go every day. She and the other women left the dorms at dawn. There were White Suits inside but we never saw them. They did not enter The Shed through the big gate that was for the women's use. They had their own door at the back, through the Sick Room. As we were growing up, the presence of White Suits inside The Shed became a common knowledge, and as time passed, it was a knowledge that completely terrified me.

5 MEMORIES OF MY ONE AND ONLY SNEAK PEEK INTO THE SHED

In spite of being strictly out of bounds, I came close to visiting inside The Shed once, and it was enough to last me a lifetime. It was the day Rosichi's mom didn't come back to the dorms. Rosichi got really worried. She came to my bed when I was about to fall asleep and gave me a small nudge, but it was enough to make me jump. It was probably before I had the gift of smelling danger miles away.

"What the heck, Rosichi!" I could feel my heart pounding.

"Sorry Sunny," her whispers were always so loud, she could just as well talk with her normal voice it wouldn't have made a difference. "I don't think my mom came back from The Shed. Can it be? How can it be?"

"What do you mean, 'did not come back'? Are you sure?"

"Almost sure… I didn't see her, and I was told to shoo off from the women's dorms when I went looking. I'm scared Sunny. I don't think my mom's back!"

"Maybe she is just late or something?" I said as I yawned. I didn't mean to yawn, it just sort of escaped.

Rosichi started weeping.

"Sunny, you are my best friend. You have to help me find her!"

I couldn't let her down.

Sneaking around after lights out was utterly forbidden. We were not allowed out of the dorms unless there was some serious reason to, like if a fire broke out, or as I later realized, you sense a raid on the farm from miles away. If you got caught outside you were in deep trouble.

"Of course I'll help you. Come with me."

We tiptoed down the stairs. It was dark outside but the yard in front of the dorms was lit.

"Let's go from the back," I said.

The girls' dorm was an old building that a long time ago, before my time, was brightly painted. It stood horizontally to the other two dorm buildings. We tiptoed behind it very quietly, walking all the way to the south end. From there, we ran through the gap between the girls' dorm and the babies'. The babies' dorm was a single level building that was only slightly more cheerful looking than the other two. Babies were all sleeping in one single room in their cribs.

Normally two or three women were present there with the babies at any given time. But not the mothers of those babies. The mothers were rarely allowed inside to visit. I remember how Mom was desperate to visit Precious. She was screaming at those women to let her in and see her baby. But they did not let her. They were heavy duty thugs those women. They had wooden bats and they were not afraid to use them.

I saw one of my mom's friends get beaten up once. They truly whacked her up. She was bleeding everywhere. I'm not sure what happened to her. I haven't seen her again in the farm and no one dared speak of it, ever.

Girls were allowed to go in with the babies, so Mom used to send me in there, to look after Precious. Each time I came out, I had to go back to Mom and tell her everything. How was Precious? Was she happy? Was she smiling? Did she recognize me? Was she growing up nicely? I wasn't that keen on those visits. Not that I didn't like to see Precious. I loved to see her. She was the sweetest little baby you could ever imagine. She recognized me for sure. She really smiled for me every time I came in. But I hated the interrogation by my mom afterwards. She was so desperate. I think she lost a bit of that desperation with Antim. The fire was out.

Rosichi and I snuck behind the babies' dorms and ran past the gap to the eastern wall of the women's dorms. I had to check that Rosichi's mom wasn't there. I thought I could start by asking my mom if she knew anything.

We had to get to the front of the women's dorms to go in but the front of the building was lit and I was scared that we might be seen by the "Patrol". The Patrols were made of women who were watching the buildings at night. These women at the same time both were and weren't part of our community. They lived amongst us and all, and we knew them by their names, but like the women in the babies' dorms, these women were not strictly partaking in the community. They had their own room in the women's dorms at the bottom floor by the entrance, and they sat separately from us in the community room during meals or whenever we used it. They rarely engaged in a conversation with anyone else expect their own little group. And they could be quite harsh with the wooden bat as I already told you. Maybe once when they were younger they were part of the community, who knows. Maybe they grew up here. We didn't know and we didn't really want to know.

We squatted at the front east corner and checked for Patrols. The thought of getting caught under those ferocious bats was terrifying. Rosichi started pulling at my sleeve. Ahead of us a Patrol was coming closer. The two women were talking to each other and not paying much attention. We didn't have many sneaking arounds at the farm, so maybe they just got a bit careless with time.

We backtracked carefully and ran back to hide behind the women's dorms, panting. There was no way to get in through the front door. I knew where my mother's room was. It was on the second floor, third little window from the right. I looked up the building.

"Let's throw stones at the window," I suggested.

We picked up little stones from the ground and tried to throw them at my mother's window. We did a terrific job at missing it every time. My last throw hit bullseye on the window second from the right. I held my breath and felt a cold shiver come over me. In the darkness I could just see a woman's face coming close to the window. Instantly I grabbed Rosichi and pushed both of us to the wall. It was very dark and I was nearly sure the woman at the second-floor window could not have seen us, but I was scared nevertheless. I don't remember how long we just stood there like that, frozen to the wall. I thought I could hear steps above us. In my terrified mind I could just envision the woman from the window telling The Patrol that there were suspicious movements downstairs. That would be the end of us. But after a while everything went quiet again. No Patrol came and we started breathing normally again. There was no point throwing any more stones. I checked up the wall closely. There was no way I could have climbed up to my mother's window.

Rosichi looked at me, defeated. "We should go back, Sunny. It's not going to work."

"Hell, no." I said. I don't know why I said that. Of course we should have gone back and forgotten about the whole thing. In the morning we could have asked my mom where Rosichi's mom was. But no. Me and my quick automatic responses. "We'll go to The Shed."

"Are you *insane?*" Rosichi was whispering so loudly it couldn't truly be considered whispering.

Surely I had lost my wits just suggesting that.

"Do you have a better idea?" I said, perhaps a little too harshly. I softened my tone, "Do you want to see where your mom is or not?"

Rosichi hesitated. You could tell she was scared. Really scared. So was I.

"OK," she said finally. "We'll just get close.... But we won't go in, Sunny!"

We tiptoed behind the community room and the kitchen until we got to the corner end of that block, just behind the community room's toilets. There were no more buildings between us and The Shed. Darkness stretched ahead of us. The wind was harsher than usual. The crickets' chirps in the fields sounded more like alarm sirens piercing the night. But above all else I could hear the wild drumming of my heartbeat. I took a deep breath.

"Ready to run?" I asked Rosichi. She didn't even have time to answer, I just grabbed her hand and ran for it.

We ran as fast as we could under the cover of darkness until we were nearly lined up with The Shed, just coming at it from the south side. We nearly made it, when my foot caught onto something sharply protruding from the ground and I stumbled and dived head first to the ground. I tried very hard not to yell. I bit my lips trying desperately to muffle the groan that was brewing to escape. Rosichi was at my side, her hands on my shoulder, whispering nervously, and rather loudly, "Sunny, are you OK?.. Sunny...?"

I was lying on the ground. I had hit my face and my side. It probably wasn't quite as bad as it felt; more than anything, I think it was the shock of falling out of the blue that had knocked the wind out of me.

Stupid, stupid, stupid. I should have remembered the graves.

To the side of The Shed, far from the dorm buildings but close enough to see them, that's where we buried our dead. It was a small section of mostly grass where the soil was soft and compliant. The girls made small plaques for the departed loved ones who died. That was how we paid our respects. Nothing fancy. I remember I made the plaque for Precious. Heck, it might even have been her plaque I stumbled on.

I could feel some blood trickling from my nose. I was putting all my efforts into keeping quiet. But my fall probably made quite the THUD anyway, and the Patrol was on us in a flash.

That's it. We're dead, I thought.

"What's going on there? What are you doing there?" The two women on The Patrol sounded extremely unfriendly. I could barely talk. I could see from their silhouettes that one of them was Anne. A short, big bosomed woman, who used to wear her hair cropped very short. I didn't know much about Anne. Was she nice? Was she about to beat me to death with her bat? I didn't know... I was about to find out. My pulse was so hysterically high I felt my heart might jump out of my mouth if I opened it. But then, out of the blue Rosichi did something really amazing.

"Thank goodness you found us! I was so worried! Oh, thank goodness, thank goodness!"

She sounded scared and nervous and sincere all at the same time. I was a little shocked by that performance, as I was not quite sure where she was going with it.

"Sunny got feeling so bad, she was nearly rolling off her bad with stomach pain and I just was so worried and I decided to take her to the Sick Room... but I couldn't see the way and she fell... she is so unwell... we need to go to the Sick Room. Please!"...

I thought Rosichi was being rather brilliant. But also, more than a little reckless.

The Sick Room was adjacent to The Shed, right at the back of it. It had three entry points: one from the south side, through which the girls in the farm used to enter it. The second one was at the west side of the building, through which the White Suits came in. And the third one was an internal door that linked The Shed to the Sick Room. We never entered the Sick Room on our own. We were completely banned from using any other door but the south side one. And we certainly were never ever supposed to sneak to the Sick Room after lights out.

"Is this Sunny?" Anne asked.

"Uuhuuugh," I groaned.

"You are Stella's girl?" she asked.

"Ahhhuhhh," I groaned and nodded as best I could. "Yeah," I said, a little clearer.

The other woman, a taller one whose hand was at the ready on her wooden bat came very close to Rosichi. She shouted at her from so close a distance it seemed she might just eat up Rosichi's nose.

"Don't you know this is FORBIDDEN? Are you stupid, Girl?"

"No, no, no, no I know, I know it's forbidden, I know." She was talking so fast I could tell she was just completely freaking out "But... but my friend... she is my best friend... she isn't well... I got... er... really really scared..."

"Why didn't you come to us then, Girl?" the other woman who was not Anne asked Rosichi. "Why did you NOT COME to US?"

"I don't know, I don't know... I didn't want to make any noise... I was just... her mom... she lost the child you know... and she might have become... you know... upset!"

Anne kneeled by my side. "Can you walk?" I nodded, although I wasn't sure. I was so taken with Rosichi's performance I wasn't sure about much anymore.

Anne put her hand firmly under my arm.

"Anne… we shouldn't,"… the other woman was trying to say.

"We can't leave her here," Anne said.

In one strong push she heaved me up on my feet. My head was dizzy and I felt like vomiting.

"OK. Let's take you to the Sick House" she said to me. "But you," she turned to Rosichi. "You are going back to your bed, Girl."

Rosichi was trying to say something, to insist, but the other woman just pushed her away.

"I'll be fine Rosichi," I said as reassuringly as I could, as I was dragged one way by Anne and Rosichi was pushed away the other.

We entered the Sick Room through the Girls' entrance door. The Sick Room was a large building, as large as The Shed and it was divided internally into rooms and sections. When you entered the Sick Room from the Girls' south side door, there was no way you could see into the section which had the door to The Shed. It was locked. Out of reach.

Anne turned the lights on and sat me on a tired little stool in the corner of the room.

"I'll get some water and a clean towel," she said. "We'll clean your face and the bleeding first."

She unlocked the door on the other side of the room and disappeared.

I took a good look around. I knew that if Rosichi's mom was there, the Sick Room entrance would not be the room she would be in. It would be one of the internal rooms, one of those rooms that I was not allowed to go to under any circumstances.

The room used to be white but the walls now had stains, hand prints, some blood stains even. It was a gloomy place. It was not my first time there of course, but I can't say that I visited it often. Like most girls, I had the odd sore throat, the odd 'flu. Once I had an ear infection and once I sprained my ankle. The visits were always brief. I was usually seen by a woman of The Patrol and only once, very very briefly, a White Suit saw me. That was when I sprained my foot. I nearly got a heart attack when the White Suit walked in to have a look at my leg. It was a man. He had latex gloves on, and he wore glasses. He had streaks of grey in his hair, which was a little curly at the back. "Damaged Goods, are we?" he joked, as he touched my leg and twisted it here and there. I was so darn shocked I didn't even wince. "Hmmm… no. Not broken," he said, and left the room. That was so weird. It was the only time I came that close to a White Suit. Normally it was just the Patrol.

There were a few posters on the walls. They were weird. Promoting all kinds of foods and medicines I have never even once seen on the farm. All sorts of weird looking foods, I don't even know what they were. To be honest, some of them kind of reminded me of what one might leave in the toilet. One poster always grabbed my attention more than any of the others. It was a little worn and chipped on the edges, and it might have known better days before the colors faded off it a bit, but I was always drawn to it, like a magnet. On this poster there was a family. A girl, a boy, a mother and a father. This in itself was strange. We had no boys in the farm. Never. I hadn't even seen a boy in my entire life. We only saw them in the old books we had in the community room. So, I knew they looked a little different than girls, and they had a penis, and they loved football and they loved nice cars. That's what the books said. But more strangely… we had no fathers in the farm.

All the girls were desperate to know who their father was and where he was, but none more so than me, or so it seemed. At least for a while. I must have been only four seasons old. I used to haunt my mom after she came back from The Shed asking and asking, "Just tell me his first name." "Did you meet on the farm?" "Has he ever seen me?" "Is he Precious's dad too?" She used to get very angry with me, and the more I asked, the more frustrated she became. "But why? Why won't you tell me? Why?"

I pestered my mother so badly asking about my father she slapped me on the face once. My cheek burned for several hours, but my insult was burning even worse. I never asked her about him again. I kept thinking that one day I'll set Precious at her to do the questioning for me. But then Precious died, and one day mom got pregnant again. The baby was born dead I was told. It was a boy. But when mom got pregnant *again* I was pretty sure by then that it wasn't by my dad because, I figured, if he came all the way here to see my mom and get her pregnant, then why did he not ask to see me?

That other baby was also born dead. He was a boy.

Anne returned to the room. She broke my fixation with the poster. "That's a nice-looking family, ain't it?" she said, about the man, woman, boy and girl in the poster. "All smiling and happy looking," she said. I nodded. The family in the poster were certainly displaying some oddly big smiles and unnaturally white teeth. I would say they looked smug. They were all holding drinking glasses like they were just about to toast them together, and the glasses were filled to the brim with this white stuff. The words said "Natures. The REAL taste."

Anne patted my face with the towel. Then she stood me up on my feet. My side still hurt. She lifted my shirt up. I was not expecting that and felt a little embarrassed.

"There's nothing here I haven't seen before, Girl," she said, half-jokingly.

She did not seem mad. Not very cruel either. I was pretty sure by then that she was not about to beat me to death. She pressed my ribs. It hurt, but not as much as I thought it might.

"I need a different bandage," she mumbled to herself. "Stay here."

She went out of the room again. I watched her go through the door… and then… she left it open! The door to the inner room was left open! I must have knocked my head pretty badly because I started walking towards the open door. My body was sore and my shirt was still up. My hand shook with nerves as I came close to the gap the door left. I peeked through. First, I only put the tip of my nose in, expecting Anne to come running at me, slamming the door in my face. But the room was quiet. I stretched my neck and put my entire head through. Beyond the door was another white washed room, a little smaller than the one I was just in. It had a funny looking bed that looked nothing like the ones we have at the dorm, and some cupboards and a shiny small table with lots of drawers. There were tubes and needles on the table, a little scattered. The room was empty and quiet. Anne was not in there. But from one side I could see all the way to the other, and I caught my breath to find that the door on the far side of the second room was also wide open. It was almost like I was invited to come through.

I walked into the second room, making small, quiet steps. In many ways it was just like the other one. It had silly posters on its walls too. There was one with a blonde woman, looking healthy and sporty, smiling widely, wearing funny white clothes and a white band around her forehead. "Natures. The REAL taste."

The bed was slightly curved up and it had funny looking, pedal-like legs. I touched the pedals; they were ice cold, and they squeaked. It was only a tiny little metallic squeak but in the complete silence of the place, in the emptiness of it, it seemed to be magnified to an immense noise. I stopped in my tracks right there, cold sweat forming on my forehead. Anne was bound to come in and kill me. I just waited for it to happen. I knew that was it for me, right there in that boring, white room, with that stupid looking bed, where Rosichi's mom was not hiding, and where I saw absolutely nothing, nothing of interest.

But Anne did not rush into the room. In fact, she was nowhere to be seen.

I kept walking in, deeper into the room. Getting closer and closer to the other door. And then, I was there. By that door. On the verge of going deeper into the Sick Room than I'd thought was possible. I peeked inside. The next room was small and narrow. It looked like a storage room. There were all sorts of tools and machineries in it. Some machines had "on" and "off" buttons and some had "Automated" switches. Funny looking machines that looked like the mythological sea creatures with tentacles that I'd seen in books. The wall on the other side was made of glass. Through it I was able to see into a hall which lead to yet another door, a sliding door, the inner door to The Shed.

I sneaked slowly to the window and carefully looked through. I could make out very little, as I was still too far away and only shot it a quick glance, too scared to be found out by Anne. Of what I'd seen, The Shed was very mechanical. The walls were an odd shade of green, grimy looking, and there were some sort of seating stations, with machines at each station. I could not tell what these machines did. It looked so weird. I couldn't understand what was done there. Why was my mom coming here every day? It was so odd. It didn't seem like a place where anyone would be doing any sort of work that I was familiar with.

Then, at the corner of the far side of that corridor, I could just make out a White Suit coming through The Shed. I dropped to the floor, catching my breath. I was hoping against hope that I was not seen. I looked around in complete panic. Why was I here? What a stupid idea it was to come here! And where was Anne? I needed to get out of there, to crawl on my aching knees and elbows, just get out of there! As my eyes glanced around, my sight fell on a row of peculiar jars all orderly placed side by side on the shelf. Looking up at them from the floor where I was crouching, they seemed utterly terrifying. As I was sorting my breath, trying to get my thoughts in order, I tried to focus on those jars, to understand what was in them. There were things floating in gross-looking brown tinted water. They looked like little babies. But that wasn't possible… surely. I raised myself only a smidgen from the floor as I got closer to look at them more clearly. I had to put my hand on my mouth to choke the shriek that was about to escape it. Rows and rows of big jars with dead babies floating aimlessly in them. Some babies were large, the size I remembered Precious was when she was born. Others were smaller. But they were all perfectly formed. Their faces seemed slightly swollen. And there was something else… they did not seem peaceful. Like they hated it. As if floating in gooey water in jars was not something they particularly enjoyed. I looked at them, while in the back of my head I was screaming at my feet, "Run! Get out of here!" but I couldn't stop looking. Then it hit me. They were all boys. All of these babies floating in jars were boys. An ominous feeling snuck into the pit of my stomach. Every jar had a sticker and there were scribbles on each one. I looked at them.

Stella. Boy. Full term

Stella. Boy. 34 weeks

Stella. Boy. 28 weeks

Stella. Boy. Full term.

I felt like I was about to puke on the floor. My head was so dizzy I had to hold on to the shelf. The walls were closing in. I could hear the White Suit talking to Anne somewhere near enough that they might find me here any minute. Any second now.

With my final energy reserves I ran out of that room, through the door to the small room with the funny bed, through the other door to the first room with the stupid family poster. I ran outside and I kept running. I ran past the second Patrol Woman, the one that pushed Rosichi back to the dorms. She was shouting something at me in a very angry voice, but I did not stop. I just kept running, past the community room, past the women's dorms, past the babies' dorms, up the stairs and into my room. I dived into my bed and got under the duvet. My body was still sore and I was shaking all over.

I was not thinking of Rosichi's mom at all. All I could think of were

42

those jars. The baby boys. My mom's name on each one of them. And one more thing. All the jars had had another sticker. A colorful little thing. It said "Natures".

I was half expecting a firing squad to meet me in the morning. But there was no firing squad. Not even Patrol Woman Anne came to look for me. Only Rosichi. Shaken, I told her about what I'd seen. We were so terrified, we agreed to never speak of that night again with anyone. Anyone at all. I regretted this agreement the very next day when I saw my mom. I wanted so desperately to ask her about the jars. What did they mean? Were they real babies? *Her* children? *My* brothers? Why? Why were they there? What was the meaning of this place? Why did she never tell me?

But I never went back on a promise, so I did not utter a word.

*

Rosichi's mom never came back. She was gone. Not even my mom spoke of her, and they were supposed to be friends.

*

Ever since that night The Shed cast such a dark cloud over me, I was reluctant to even visit the graves. It scared me beyond words. I sometimes awoke at night with nightmares of babies floating in jars. The place was wicked and bizarre. I just could not figure out why we even had it there, in the farm, where life was altogether peaceful otherwise.

And now, now my mom sent me to find Rosichi and to run away, but Snotty just said that Rosichi went to The Shed with the other older girls.

No matter however which way I tossed it over in my head, it was bad.

6 INTO THE SHED – THIS TIME FOR REAL

The memories of that night, my sneak peek into The Shed, were still very vivid in my mind. Even though many months had passed since then, I still had nightmares of babies in jars. So now, facing The Shed again, being *ordered* to go in, out of all things, seemed to be a completely insanity.

Every muscle in my body was screaming to me not to go, but there was no other way around it. To get Rosichi I had to follow her into The Shed. What the heck was she thinking, going there, anyway? After everything I'd told her about what I'd seen all those months ago. And without even making sure I was there with her... without even calling me. I was confused, a little angry. A little disappointed. But mostly, I was afraid. Why were all the girls taken to The Shed? Normally only the women would go. Never us. Never the young girls.

But... maybe... we weren't so young any more. I was nearly fifteen and Rosichi too, even though she looked so much younger.

Five months before that morning in the Kale garden, I had my first bleeding. I was so scared initially. Some of the girls had had their bleeding already for months and longer, so I knew what it was all about. But just taking down my undies at the toilet and seeing the smudge of blood on them was a bit scary. I kept the promise I made to Mom the day after the raid, and went to tell her that very evening.

"I started my bleeding," was all I had to say. She had her serious face on. She gave me a hug. A big hug. "It's going to be OK," she said. Then she took me to the women's dorms and gave me some pads to put on my undies to protect them. And that was it.

So, we were not little girls any more. Most of us were wearing bras, and had our bleedings… maybe the ban on entering The Shed was about to be lifted for the girls in my age group? I was not sure. I had no desire to get into that place, but I had no other choice either. So, I ran. I ran in the direction I wanted to run to the least. Straight into The Shed. I wasn't sure how to get in. Do I bang on the door of The Shed? Or do I go around and bang on the door of the Sick Room? Which door do I need to kick to get Rosichi out? I really had no time to think it through. So, I just ran to the main door of The Shed and started banging on the door.

"Let me in!" I screamed like I'd lost my mind "Rosichi!!! Are you in there?" I banged the door with everything I had.

There was no movement. The door remained shut. Nothing was happening.

"LET. ME. IN!" I shouted again and again. "Rosichi!! Open the door!" … "Open!"…

Then something in my mind switched and I shouted, "This is Sunny. I am Stella's girl!"

First there was nothing and I thought that I'd probably missed my chance. I would not be able to get Rosichi and run far away. I'd blown it. But then the door started moving. It groaned and moaned, and slowly opened. A man in a white suit stood there looking at me.

"Come inside" he said.

I caught my breath. So, I just walk in there? The place of nightmares? I didn't really have any choice. I had to get Rosichi out of there. So I walked in.

The door slammed shut behind me.

The first thing I noticed was the sound. The sound and the smell. It was so off-putting, so sour and rotten, combined with the horrific noise, it created such a profound vertigo effect on me. There was nothing to hold on to but air so I just tried desperately to remain calm and keep my wits. The sound was an assault on the ears. It was so foreign to any other sound I recognized, so soul piercing and alien that it had an almost blinding effect. The sounds of machines pumping and sucking and whooshing and gurgling. FFFFFFFFFFFF… Shshshshshshshshsh… FFFFFFFFFF… shshshshshshshshshshs…

The lights inside The Shed were rather dim, coming from the brightness of the outside world, it took me a while to adjust. It was one thing taking a glimpse of The Shed from the Sick Room, and another thing entirely standing right in it. An entirely different perspective. It was an enormous space, filled to the brim with machines. Everything, including the floor, had a faded color of what must have once been a rather cheerful green but now was moldy and dirty and stained and miserable, a color like vomit. The room was divided to stations. Rows and rows and rows of them. Each station had a sort of weird looking chair with lots of straps, and all the chairs were hooked to those sucking machines. The machines were the only things not colored vomit green. They had strange tentacles that looks like slim feeble hands, only at the end of each tentacle, instead of palms, they had some sort of cups.

I strained my eyes to see better. I had to act quickly, but where was Rosichi? I couldn't see any of the girls. What I did see, at one of the far corners of the room, was that some of the stations were occupied. I stared ahead, attempting to focus, to be able to understand what I was looking at. Suddenly I realized what I was seeing and my stomach twisted in a tight fearful knot. I recognized what was occupying those stations. They were women. Women of the farm community. Mom's friends.

I saw Freckles. I was certain it was her. You couldn't miss Freckles from any distance; even in The Shed her hair was orange. She was half naked. Her blouse was off. She seemed to be strapped to the chair around her head, hands and feet. Her head was sort of lopsided, like she was trying to look very hard at something to the side of her, or maybe she was sleeping. But since I have the gift of smelling danger a mile away, I could definitely sense that Freckles wasn't sleeping. Something was definitely not right with her. I needed to vomit.

Her naked bosom was not visible. She had those tentacles attached to her. Each breast was held in a cup, each cup was attached to those metallic tentacles. The tentacles were attached to the sucking machine and were twirling and wiggling like they were dancing with her breasts inside them. The view was so grotesque and so absurd, I could actually feel my jaw dropping. Tentacles having a party… sucking Freckles' life out.

Was she dead? I wanted to scream to her, "Freckles! Freckles!" but the White Suit grabbed my right arm so suddenly, it knocked all my intentions and all that momentary bravery out of me.

The White Suit turned my arm to have the soft side up. He wasn't even trying to be gentle about it. He twisted my arm as if it wasn't even attached to me. It hurt. I gave a small squeal. He didn't bother apologizing. He didn't even look at me, only at my arm. Then he felt with his other hand at the side of my wrist. I was annoyed. I wanted to pull my arm out of his grasp but he held it so tightly that I didn't dare. He then took a strange machine from his pocket. It was a small, black, hand-held device with some sort of electronic face to it. He hovered the device over my wrist. The machine gave a small "beep" sound like it recognized something inside my hand. Something under my skin, inside my flesh. Despite my wish, I was mesmerized by this. Was there something there? Inside me? Something that the White Suit could so easily find?

"You're ready," he said, and pushed me forward.

My feet felt like they weighed a ton. Each one. My stomach was in a knot. My breath heavy and unsteady. But there was something else there too. A bit of defiance. A bit of rebellion. A bit of courage. My brain was in turmoil. So many contradicting messages were assailing me that I thought I would be gone half mad before I had a chance to do anything *"Go!... Stay!... Run!... Find Rosichi!... Run to Freckles!... Run away!... How?... Push the White Suit! Kick him!... Are you stupid? Do what he says!"....*

The White Suit was walking next to me. He didn't push me or talk to me or even look at me. His presence there was enough. I kept walking deeper and deeper into The Shed. I still could not see any of the girls.

But then, we crossed a row of those tentacle stations that were bunched together like an island in the center of our path, and beyond it the view of that section of the room had opened up to us in a matter of steps. Suddenly I saw women. Nearly all of the women I knew from the farm. Mothers of my friends and some whose children were younger than me. They were all sitting on those evil looking chairs, their foreheads, stomachs, hands and feet strapped.

They were all half naked and their breasts were being sucked by the wobbly tentacles, whooshing and FFFFFFFFsing, dancing their jolly dance. All of them seemed to be unconscious somehow... their eyes were open but they were just gazing, just staring aimlessly into the room, not focused on anything. None of them saw me, none of them recognized me. No one spoke.

The smell was putrid and I gagged. I had to stop in my tracks not to throw up right there on the floor. I felt dizzy.

"Keep going," the White Suit said.

"Are they dead?" I asked, even though I knew full well they were alive. I could see them breathe. I just didn't know what was happening to them. Why were they like this?

The White Suit did not respond. We do not talk to the White Suits, only listen. I guess he wasn't used to being talked to.

Out of nowhere another White Suit entered the room. They all looked so much like each other. I really don't know how they could tell each other apart.

The other White Suit was holding a pad of papers and had a pen stuck behind his ear. He placed himself at the side of one of the women being sucked. I knew her well, it was Alberta. Her daughter, Maisy, was born on the same season with Precious. But unlike Precious, Maisy did not die, she was still there, outside, possibly playing with her friends. Mom liked Maisy but every time she saw her, a feather-light shudder went through her, so small that only I knew it to recognize. I realized that what my mom saw was not only Maisy but also Precious, or what Precious might have been. To my mom, Maisy was Maisy but she was also the ghost of Precious. Poor girl.

The other White Suit was checking Alberta. He placed his fingers on the side of her neck. He was staring into the panel of the machine to which the tentacles were attached. The panel displayed various numbers, lights and odd signals. He took some notes down. He touched her again, grabbing her cheeks and turning her head from side to side, very roughly, while shining a light from the tip of his pen into her eyes.

The White Suit that was walking next to me was quickening his pace, probably due to the fact that he was reluctant to allow me to be exposed to the scene further, beyond what I was already exposed to. But I had to see more. I had to understand what was going on. I measured my steps by only a fraction, so that now I was falling behind.

The White Suit near Alberta pressed on a switch and in an instant the jolly tentacles fell limp and silent. The White Suit put his notes down on the top of the panel, and used both his hands twisting the cup that held Alberta's left breast. As the cup released from holding the breast I could see Alberta's reddened breast sort of dropping back onto her torso. Her nipple brown and large, and there was white liquid dripping out of it. I mean, really dripping… down her tummy and onto the floor. It made me shudder. I wanted to avert my eyes but I couldn't. I needed to understand what was happening to Alberta, but no matter how hard I looked, it still didn't make sense.

The man was looking into the cup and giving it a bit of a wipe. He was observing Alberta's breast. Touching it, squeezing it. I didn't like it. It made me feel rather angry, seeing her touched like that, still strapped and gazing aimlessly, not able to defend herself. It wasn't right. Is this what happens to Mom every time she came here? I gagged again. I couldn't help it. What the heck was this place?

The White Suit that was leading me realized I was walking deliberately slowly and watching Alberta. He stopped, returned to me and grabbed me by the arm very firmly. He wasn't even pretending to be nice. "Come!" he said.

I had to speed up. My arm was locked in his hand. We passed Alberta's station and she disappeared from my view. Other women filled stations all along the path and in little central islands. The smell was giving me a headache.

We approached a corner of the room, where I could spot the entrance to the Sick Room, but instead of going through it into the Sick Room the White Suit turned right and kept walking along the wall until we reached another door, this one just a simple door, not endowed with heavy locks as the others. He knocked first then turned the knob and opened the door.

It was an inner room. There was nothing in it. Nothing but girls.

7 DEEPER INTO THE SHED WE GO

Instantly I saw Rosichi standing in the back of the room, her own arm around herself. She welcomed me with a bright smile that shone against the room, but then in a flash, her smile faded.

The White Suit pushed me aggressively into the room. There was another White Suit inside with my friends. The two men exchanged some words in a hushed tone, then the White Suit that took me there left and closed the door behind him.

All eyes were on me. Some girls nodded. There were murmurs. I could clearly hear one of them saying, "Stupid!" at me. Nice.

I walked straight to Rosichi.

"What are you doing here, Sunny?" she asked, with her not-quite-under-control loud whispering voice.

"What do you mean, what am I doing here?" I was thrown aback by her question. "I came to find you!" I looked around to make sure no White Suit was hiding beside us. "I came to rescue you."

"Why? Are you stupid? I was telling them you were on the other side of the farm so they don't come looking for you! You were *safe!*"

The way she said 'safe!' was like a challenge to a duel, not like someone who was actually looking for my safety.

"Who is 'they'? Why would anybody be looking for me? I wasn't at the pond. I was at the Kales. You know that."

"Are you serious? … *Of course* I knew that! … But I didn't want them to take you too!" She sighed, then said in a rather judgmental voice, "*I* was trying to rescue *you!*"

"What do you mean 'take me too'?" I felt like there was more than a bit of information that I was missing there. "What happened today?"

Rosichi rolled her eyes. Then she told me. They came suddenly. A rather large group of White Suits assisted by about four of those rigid, bullying, beat-the-heck-out-of-you Patrol women. They spread out around the living compound and rounded all the older girls. The younger girls were sent to the community room.

"They used this hand-held machine to check our wrists," she said, showing me the location on her arm.

"I know. They checked me when I came in here," I said. "Did you ever feel something was inside there? Some sort of… I don't know… a machine of some kind?" I asked her.

"No… never," she said.

Rosichi got back to her story. They were gathered in front of the women's dorms. They were searched and their arms were checked.

"The White Suits knew immediately they were missing a few," she said, "and it seems like they knew exactly who was missing, which is strange because they don't even know our names or anything. I suppose it's because of the machines that are inside our arms."

Monica was found in the laundry inside the women's dorms. They found Flower in the orchard.

"There were some discussions and a lot of counting and looking at papers. So, I just went to Anne, the Patrol Woman who is actually the nicest one of them all, and I just said to her that if it was you they were still looking for, that you were at the pond." Rosichi was truly a fantastic liar.

"I didn't think they'd believe me, she said, "but I guess they did because they didn't continue looking for you. They just kept us all hanging there waiting while they got your mom out of The Shed."

The White Suits got my mom out of The Shed and ordered her to find me and get me inside the Sick Room as soon as possible.

"This is a vile place, Sunny," Rosichi said. "I never understood what they were doing here and what all the secrecy was about. But now that I've seen it I don't want to know!"

I nodded in agreement.

Rosichi looked at me with a rather sad look. "So, she looked for you? She actually looked for you and sent you here?"

I knew she was talking about my mom. I knew what she was thinking. What woman in her right mind would send her own child to this place?

"She sent Snotty to get me," I answered, "but when I got to the dorms she told me to find you and to run away.... Away from the farm. That's why I followed you inside here."

Rosichi smiled a sad smile "You are very brave Sunny." She sighed and gave my hand a little squeeze. "Very brave and stupid!"

"We need to find a way out of here," I said with a shred of defiance.

"Are you blind?" Rosichi said. It was a bit hurtful, her utter lack of confidence in my ability to get us out of there.

"SILENCE THERE!" the White Suit by the door was saying at no one in particular.

"I WILL get us out of here," I said to her defiantly. I even believed it when I said it, but not so much the second after the words were uttered. I always was quick to say things that required a bit more thinking through. I had absolutely no idea how I was going to do that.

We waited in the room. There were no chairs, no water. It was getting hot and stuffy inside. I think it was Flower who snapped first.

"Why are you holding us here? We need some water!"

The White Suit looked at her, blank of any emotion.

Nothing happened for a while, we just kept standing there, waiting. Murmurs quietened. Whispers died down. We all sank into our own minds. Just waiting.

Suddenly the door opened. Two White Suits came into the room. I was surprised to see one of them was a woman. I have never seen a woman White Suit before. I never even thought that it could be possible. She was svelte with a long and very stern face. I thought she was quite pretty, however more than a little terrifying. She was fairly tall but not as tall or as pretty as my mom. She wore her dark hair rather short, above her neckline. Her sleek, fine fringe was combed to one side of her face. I couldn't take my eyes of her. A woman White Suit was the strangest thing.

They had those hand-held devices and big black pens in their hands. The woman White Suit stood up tall, and in a steady, benign, voice started giving us instructions.

"OK girls. We are going to scan your arms once again and mark your arms with these pens," she lifted the pen in her hand to show us. "You will each be given a number on your arm. Read the number and remember it. From this moment on we will be calling you by your numbers."

No one made a sound.

"Is it understood?" the woman White Suit asked.

Everyone nodded.

Then they started scanning us all. One by one arms were grabbed and stretched and black numbers were written on our skins.

The woman White Suit was the first to reach me. She grabbed my arm but her hand was not as rough as the hand of the man who scanned me before. Her hand was a little cold. I looked at her intently. Her lips were very pink. She was a bit too gaunt, I thought. She had a faint smell of perfume, masking an elusive whiff of sweat. She did not look at me at all. She just grabbed the pen and wrote on my arm. "This is your number: One. One. Five. Seven. Two." I nodded, but she wasn't even waiting for my response. She just moved on to Rosichi.

I looked at my arm. The numbers were black and thick and alien. I had a name. My name was Sunny. Why can't they call me Sunny?

When all of the girls were scanned and marked, the woman White Suit talked to us again.

"When we call your number, you will be coming with us. If you weren't called, you will stay here until we call you."

She started reading numbers out of a sheet. "Raise your hands if your numbers were called," she said, looking at no one in particular. Ten girls raised their hands. Flower was among them. She wasn't such a close friend of mine but she was an okay girl. I felt sorry for her to be among the first group to be called. None of us had the faintest idea where they were taking us. I wondered if they were going to strap us to those seats and put those tentacled cups on our breasts. It made little sense given that some of us barely had any breasts at all…

Time went by. I was getting tired. Really tired. Then, a White Suit came into the room and called ten more numbers. Ten more girls were escorted out of the room.

There was more space to sit down now. I leaned against the wall and slid down onto the floor. Rosichi sat beside me. We didn't talk.

The room started to empty when the woman White Suit came in again. We stood up, waiting to hear the numbers called. Ten more meaningless, faceless numbers were called. I looked at my arm to make sure I didn't miss my own set of numbers being announced. I was left out again. But my breath went icy cold as I sensed Rosichi's arm going up beside me. I looked at her with terror. We can't split up! We can't! We have to stay together… what… what…. I didn't even think about what I was doing… I just raised my hand.

The woman White Suit was rather surprised to count eleven hands raised.

"I am certain I only read ten numbers. The one girl whose number I didn't call, please take your hand *down!*" She said the word 'down' with quite the venom.

I kept my hand up. I was still thinking what to do. I was so lost.

The woman White Suit strode across the room directly to me. She knew. She knew I was not called. They knew all of us. They were doing this all on purpose.

The woman White Suit faced me. Now all of a sudden, she was looking me directly in the eye. Her previously benign voice turned menacing. She put her cold hand on my neck, like she was going to choke me. "One. One. Five. Seven. Two. You are not on my list. You are not called at this time. Take your hand down. If you try to be funny one more time you will be severely punished. Do you understand?"

She pressed on my neck. Her lips were pressed tight together. She was scaring me. I took my hand down.

All I could do was watch Rosichi being walked out of the room. We got separated again. I had no idea where she was being taken while I was stuck there in the room, as far from running away as one could be.

8 THE PROCEDURE

I don't know how long I waited, maybe only several minutes again, but it certainly felt like hours. I felt deflated. All my bravado left me. I felt as if no matter what happened now, I'd just let it.

Then, from the depth of defused energy, I realized the door had opened again and numbers were being called. I vaguely realized my number was being spoken. I raised my hand, hoping I didn't mess it up again… Maybe I'd got it wrong?

I didn't get it wrong. It really was my number.

In a group of ten we walked out. The White Suit led us out of The Shed and into the Sick Room through the internal door. We were in the big hall I saw that night through the glass window of the small room. But we kept going and turned right. We walked to the far end of the hall. There was a chain of rooms on both sides. We were shown inside one of them. As we walked in I saw there were some stools and shelves. There were hooks on the walls. I swallowed hard. Under each stool there were shoes. Familiar shoes. And on the hooks

THE SHED

hung shirts and tunics I knew very well. On the shelves were pants and skirts folded neatly. I knew them all. I saw them every day.

"Take off all your clothes and set them nicely. Shoes on the floor, shirts and tunics on the hooks. Pants and skirts on the shelves. Socks inside the shoes. Underwear including bras on the stool," the White Suit ordered. "When you are done, put those tunics on." He pointed at one of the shelves. It was stacked with plain white tunics.

No one moved. I guessed we were sort of expecting him to leave the room. We'd never taken our clothes off in the presence of a White Suit before... a man! But he wasn't moving. For a few seconds we just looked at each other, not sure what to do. He must have lost patience with us. "Do what you are told! We don't have all day!"

Clumsily, awkwardly, we took off our clothes and placed them as we were told. I snuck a glance at the White Suit. I expected him to be indifferent and not even see us, but I could have sworn that he was looking.

I put a white tunic on. It was much larger than my size and it wasn't that white. It had clearly known better days. It had old stains and smears that clung to it. It grossed me out.

"Now, each of you please put on a pair of slippers from the pile over there," he said in a blank, detached voice. His body language was screaming at us that he could not be interested in the slightest whether we did put them on or not. His hand pointed towards one of the cupboards.

How were we even supposed to find the right shoe size for us? I was not certain. As if on cue, we all rushed to the cupboard, huddled and jumbled, hands reaching over hands, shoes grabbed, shoes snatched from other hands, shoes tossed over heads. You would have thought there was a reward for getting them first. I managed to grab a pair of rubbery slippers. They had a rubber band around the hem, so truly they would have fitted any size. It was not a huge surprise to find that the slippers were also the color of vile green: a complete match with the general depressing ambience of the place.

Once we were all dressed in the ghostly gowns, the White Suit ordered us to follow. We passed a few doors that were closed. I had a very strong urge to peek inside them but I didn't dare. Something inside me was still numb. Then the walls changed and instead of sealed rooms we were walking through a corridor that had glass walls on both sides. From there I could see that the path led back to the wide hall of the Sick Room that had a door to the outside. The door that was normally used by the White Suits. This had to be my escape route, I thought. Do I run for it? Now? As I am? Butt naked except this faded tunic and without Rosichi? The urge was great but I didn't do it. I don't know why, I just didn't. I guess I felt a deep desperation to find Rosichi first. Even if I made it out and ran without being caught, which was seriously doubtful, leaving without Rosichi would have been a terrible failure. One I didn't think I could have lived with.

We did not reach the hall. Instead we entered one of the large rooms with the glass walls. Its insides were divided by screens. Our group was screened off on all sides.

Inside the screened cubicle allocated to us there were two beds. Two of those funny looking beds I remembered so well with the curved shape and those metallic pedals on the edge. The ones that screeched and nearly caused me an early heart attack back then. It seemed like seasons ago, and yet, here I was again, standing near two of those beds.

The horror feeling in the pit of my stomach grew. I just knew everything to do with this room, with these beds, inside this building, was bound to be bad. Very bad.

I also realized instantly that we were not alone in the room. That other groups of girls were there, screened off just like we were. The screens shielded us from view but they couldn't cover the sounds. For White Suits, that must be rather sloppy, because we could clearly hear the whimpers and the sniffles and the quiet cries. Muffled as they were, we knew that there were girls nearby and that they were crying, only trying to hide it. Maybe with hands on their mouths or maybe they had their faces covered or something. I started to shiver. It wasn't cold in the room but I couldn't help shivering. My teeth knocked together like castanets.

Someone put a hand on my shoulder. It was Dawn. She wasn't one of my closest friends; we rarely hung out together. She was one season older than me, and I guess she never hung out with me for the same reason I never hung out with Snotty. It wasn't personal. Her hand on my shoulder was the sweetest, kindest gesture I could have asked for just then. And it took me by surprise. She smiled at me a sad little smile, probably trying to reassure me. It didn't really do the job but I was grateful to her. So I smiled a sad little smile back.

The muffled sounds from the rest of the room were very disturbing. I didn't know what was going on but on top of the whimpers and the sniffles and the hushed cries, there were gasps and sounds that indicated that pain was involved. My head was working overtime but my teeth were still knocking. I was still terrified.

The corner of the side screen was pushed to the side and a White Suit finally came inside. With him was a Patrol Woman. It wasn't Anne. This one I didn't even know by name. She did not look half as friendly as Anne. Not that Anne was that friendly either, but half of that is really nothing at all.

"From the data in our possession, you have all started having your monthly bleeding by now," the White Suit man said unceremoniously.

He wasn't asking. He was just stating a fact. How did they know that? I wasn't sure. Maybe that thing that was inside our arms told them? That meant they knew everything about us. Everything.

"This is the most exciting day in your little lives here on Natures farm," he went on as he put a vomit green latex glove on his hand, snapping it tight. "And you know why it is exciting?" he asked

66

bemusedly, then paused, as if waiting for us to figure it all out. No one answered. "It is *exciting*, because we are going to make you mommies for the very first time." He even smiled. He smiled like he'd just swallowed a lemon and was told to.

I felt like a hammer banged my head from the inside. *Your life here on Natures farm....* The posters... "Natures. The REAL taste"... the stupid family... the sporty woman. Mom's dead boys floating in jars, and the stickers that said Natures.... What was happening to us? The jigsaw was screaming at me desperately to put the pieces together, they were screaming at me, "Here we are. We are all here, put us together you silly girl!" but it still did not make any sense. *How* did it fit in? What did I possibly have in common with that stupid family in that poster? make us mommies for the very first time... I didn't want to be a mommy. I didn't want to. I wasn't ready and I was afraid... I was not ready to become my mom. What the heck was I going do? I needed to vomit. Dawn was crying. Other girls were huddled together in some sort of resistance saying, "No!" Obviously, this was not at all the most exciting day in our lives. Not at all. It was more bizarre than anything. I couldn't help but grab my head in my hands and groan. I really went for it, I groaned loudly. Not on purpose. I wasn't trying to be loud, it just came out of me. The confusion was just too much to handle.

My groan caused a chain of several things to happen.

The Patrol Woman came to me and slapped my face really hard. I mean, she put a lot of hate into that slap. The slap went on top of my own hand which was on top of my cheek so I guess it did not hurt me as much as she meant it to.

"You be quiet, Girl!" she ordered me in a growl.

The second thing was, that someone screamed from across the room, "Sunny!"

It was Rosichi. She recognized my groan. She was there.

The third thing was, that her yell to me was cut short with a loud slap. I could tell she was slapped just as hard as I was. Hard.

The fourth thing was, that the White Suit in our little curtained section nodded to the Patrol Woman and said to her, "Let's get started." From that moment things began moving very, very quickly.

I watched in horror as the Patrol Woman grabbed Dawn. I don't know why they picked her and not me. Maybe they thought she was the oldest, maybe they thought she was the leader amongst us, maybe they thought she wouldn't put up a fight. Well, they were certainly wrong there. The Patrol Woman grabbed Dawn's hand that only a moment ago was warm on my shoulder, and twisted it hard behind her back. But Dawn was fighting hard. She pushed and wriggled, she shouted and kicked. The Patrol Woman's face was getting exceedingly red. She was putting a lot of effort into bringing Dawn down. "Stop fighting!" she kept shouting at her, but the more she shouted, the more Dawn resisted.

With all the kerfuffle and the noise that was caused by the drama in our curtained section, Rosichi shouted to me again, "Sunny! Don't let them put you on the bed!" SLAP! She was shushed again.

The White Suit came over behind Dawn. He had a big syringe in his hand. With no further ado he just injected all of it into Dawn's neck. Dawn fell to the floor like a sack of potatoes. She resisted no more. They grabbed her body – the Patrol Woman grabbed the hands and the White Suit the legs and they put her on the chair. They strapped her hands to the hand rests and then they slid each leg onto one of the funny pedals, strapping her in. Then they pushed the right leg to the right and the left leg to the left, exposing her. It was the most undignified, hurtful and brutal thing that I had ever witnessed. Like she had no right to privacy. Like she was just an object. Like she meant nothing. Nothing.

I had to look away. I was horrified. They left her there like that and went back to their preparations. I glanced at the little wheeled cabinet they had at the head of the bed. There were syringes and all sorts of objects that looked alien, painful. The Patrol Woman was also putting gloves on now. "Maidenhead," the White Suit said. The Patrol woman nodded. She walked back to the position between Dawn's legs. She laid a towel underneath Dawn's bottom part. Then she sort of leaned towards Dawn's body, both hands engaged somehow. I couldn't tell what she was doing exactly. She was pushing Dawn somehow, and as she pushed she exerted this 'umph' sound, like she was making an effort. Like it took some work.

From the side of the bed, cringing with fear and disgust, I could see a small stream of blood trickling from between Dawn's legs and soaking onto the towel. After a few shoves and 'umph's the Patrol Woman looked at the White Suit who was waiting patiently for her to finish whatever it was that she was doing. She nodded at him.

She stepped away from Dawn and took off her left glove. She tossed it into a small bin by the bed.

The White Suit had a long, rubbery, tube-like syringe in his hands. It was filled with some sort of liquid. He held it very delicately, like it was precious somehow.

"Seat please," he said to the Patrol Woman. The Patrol woman nodded and rolled a small, round, wheeled seat from near the curtain to the position between Dawn's legs. Everything was happening between Dawn's legs. I wanted to vomit. My head was pounding.

The man sat himself on the little wheeled seat. Now his head was pretty much on level with Dawn's bottom half. He was pushing the syringe into Dawn's body. While one hand was engaging the syringe, the other he used to press Dawn's tummy down. One hand pressing, the other pushing. Down trickled blood onto the towel.

I don't know what came over me just then. I don't. In my mind I knew that I would definitely be next up. I knew it. I was the troublemaker all day, they had their eye on me. Before taking her, Dawn was standing next to me, she had her hand on me... It was definitely me on that stinky bed next. My head was filled with thunder and lightning. Rosichi's earlier scream to me, "Don't let them put you on the bed!" played in my head over and over... She must have seen this happening to girls in her little cubicle. Did they do it to her too? Had she already been made into a mommy? I couldn't imagine it. Rosichi looked much younger than me. Her being a mommy was surely just a twist of nature. Nature... Natures. *"Natures. The REAL taste"... the most exciting day in your little lives here on Natures farm....*

9 THE ESCAPE

I don't know what made me run. It wasn't like I made a decision to run and then started to. It wasn't like I calculated all my options and then selected the best moment to act. I just started to run. I slid under the curtain and I ran. That was all. And I did one more thing… I screamed. I screamed from the top of my lungs, "ROSICHIIIIIII!"

The commotion was immediate. It was like by my clear insane lack of obedience, I somehow managed to throw a match into a pile of twigs soaked in petrol just waiting to burn. Everyone's paralyzing fear just disappeared in an instance. Girls started screaming. Curtains were pushed aside, revealing other cubicles, other girls. Some had blood trickling down their legs and big tears smudged on their faces, some were down and out like Dawn, laying on beds with no ability to move or comprehend what was being done to them. Patrol women were running, shouting, "Stop!" and "Get back here!" Girls were running, everyone was running everywhere in every direction. It was a riot. I was just running and screaming, "ROSICHIII," like mad. Looking into cubicles, trying to avoid Patrol Women. But in my head, I knew that I was running in the wrong direction. Instead of running outside I was running in, worsening the situation and limiting my escape chances. But I had to get to Rosichi. I was almost at the last curtained cubicle when we ran straight into each other, only at the last nanosecond grabbing each other with our hands. "Sunny!" she yelled. Her voice broke. Her yell was so heart wrenching. I could hear everything that was folded into it. Her fear, her shock, her pain, her sorrow, her relief. I didn't have time to say anything at all. There was no time for conversation. I just grabbed her hand firmly in mine and started running. The place was in complete shambles. Patrol Women were grabbing screaming, kicking girls and forcing them onto beds, some girls picked up syringes and were throwing them at White Suits. Some girls were pushing the drawer cabinets across cubicles. I mean, everyone got really brave. I'm not sure what made that happen. It was like everyone's fears just went up in smoke and all the rage and humiliation surfaced instead. It was exhilarating but I had no time to dwell on it. I had to get out of there. We were so close to the door when I saw that the White Suit in charge of my cubicle was waiting there, blocking the door, a large syringe in his hand, the type he used on Dawn's neck to take her down.

I had no time to plan anything. I just kept running. We ran straight at him. Rosichi and I were not trying to coordinate anything. It's not like we were used to anything remotely similar happening to us. But maybe it was because we were both so afraid and yet so angry that we were thinking alike. We didn't need to coordinate our moves, we just knew what needed to be done and we ran for it.

We were almost at him when I released my hand from Rosichi's and grabbed the wheeled seat by Dawn's legs he'd previously sat on. The seat was much heavier than I thought it would be but I still managed to lift it in my hands and I threw it very hard at him. It was all so sudden that he didn't see it coming. He didn't even step out of the way. The chair hit him hard on his head and he fell back. He was still at the door though, blocking it, and he was still holding on to the syringe.

Rosichi rushed to his hand and tried to release the syringe from him. Hurt as he was, he still put up a good fight, strengthening his hold. He was trying to point the needle at Rosichi. "Rosichi, hold!" I shouted to her. With all her might Rosichi was trying to keep his hand still while avoiding the needle. I did the only thing that made sense. I came down close and I bit him. I bit him on the hand that was holding the syringe. I bit him so hard that he screamed and I could taste blood in my mouth. His hand opened and the syringe dropped to the floor. I could see the Patrol Woman was trying to grab it. I jumped up and kicked her as hard as I could in her knee cap. "YOU bitch!" she yelled at me as she cowered in pain. Rosichi grabbed the syringe and stuck it into the White Suit's neck. She stuck it so hard I thought the needle might come out of the other side. He just turned into a sack of potatoes. Just like Dawn.

"Sunny?" I heard a voice from nearby. It was Dawn. She was awake now. "Sunny? What happened? What happened to me?" she was asking. Her voice was weak and shaking. She was wriggling her hands that were still strapped. I wanted to release her.

"Sunny no!" Rosichi said. "No! We don't have time!"

I looked at Rosichi. Her big eyes were wide open, pleading with me. I knew she was right. We had to run. But I couldn't just leave Dawn like that.

I ran to her bed and started fiddling with the straps. They were tight. My hands were shaking and my fingers clumsy and uncoordinated. I thought it would be a piece of cake but the straps were stubborn.

"What happened to me, Sunny?" Dawn asked.

I couldn't tell her. For one, I wasn't sure myself. I just knew whatever they did was horrid, and hurtful, and abusive.

Things were starting to calm down around us. The White Suits were gaining control of the room again. I knew that the window of opportunity was closing fast.

"Rosichi, help me!" I yelled to her. But Rosichi had her own hands full. She was holding another syringe in her hands facing off another Patrol Woman who came to block the door.

I managed to unstrap Dawn's left hand and ran to her other side.

"Listen, Dawn. I will release your hands. You will need to do the legs yourself. Think you could do that?"

"Yes," she said.

Rosichi was waving the syringe at the Patrol Woman. The syringe in her right hand, her left hand holding the right hand steady. She had a look of a madwoman in her eyes.

I finally got both of Dawn's hands loose.

"Here you go, Dawn," I said.

She grabbed my arm before I managed to run off.

"Good luck!" she said to me. Her eyes looking into mine, were full of goodness, but her hand was cold now. Cold and pale.

I just gave her a quick smile and I ran. With all my might I smacked the Patrol Woman dueling with Rosichi on the back of her head. She didn't bend or fall to the ground, but she did turn around towards me, surprised, which gave Rosichi the perfect opportunity to stick her with the syringe. This one too went all the way in.

The Patrol Woman fell to the ground.

Rosichi grabbed my hand and finally we ran out of the door.

As fast as we could we ran through the hall, making our way to the large heavy door leading outside. It was the closest door to take us to the outside. Used only by the White Suits, it was the door on the western corner of the building. None of us ever got near it, not from the outside and certainly never from the inside. I had no idea what awaited on the other side of the door or what to do next, all I knew was that we had to reach the door. We had to get outside, out and away from The Shed. I could see sunlight outside, but the door was closing. Someone on the outside was closing it. Three White Suits were running after us. They were shouting "Stop them!" to two others that came through the other side of the Sick Room. One of those White Suits was the woman who choked me. We ran like mad. I don't remember ever running so fast, so focused. Not even on the night of the raid with Antim in my arms did I run so fast. I didn't feel my body. I didn't feel anything. I just ran like I was empty.

The door was closing and was now just a slim shrinking gap. Just seconds before the door closed on us we charged through it, or more like, we threw ourselves at it. We fell onto the ground rolling over. I had dirt in my mouth and I could feel Rosichi's elbow in my shoulder, as I heard the door slam and being locked shut.

The door was being locked.

It occurred to me, someone just locked the door from the *outside*.

I looked up in wonder.

Snotty was standing there. A winning smile on her face.

10 RUN!

It took me a couple of seconds to process that scene.

"Snotty?" is all I could muster. The surprise and confusion, mixed with all the horror experienced inside The Shed, and those White Suits we just managed to temporarily outrun, were all a bit too much to handle.

"Yup! That's me," she said with some real pride.

"What are you doing here? How…?" I didn't even know where to begin.

"Never mind all that. I'll tell you everything later, but we really must run. Like, NOW!" she said, and her voice lost that faint smug tone she used before, and turned into alarm.

She was right. The chase was on. This door may have been shut but there were still two other doors leading out of The Shed. In no time those White Suits would be all over us.

Rosichi was quick to jump up to her feet. Snotty reached out her hand to me to help me up, but I managed to get up without her help. To be honest, being rescued by a seven seasons old girl was quite a shock in itself. I had a lot of pride, and having her help me get up on my feet was just not something that I could deal with just then.

We started running north, towards the fields. We ran like our backs were on fire. I sensed Snotty was finding it a little difficult to keep up with us so I grabbed her hand in mine and we kept running together. My throat was burning. We had not been offered a drop of water all day, and now this frantic run was starting to take its toll on me. But I couldn't stop. There was no time. Every second mattered. I did not even stop to look back.

I expected to have White Suits running after us with all their might. I thought they might swarm out of The Shed like wasps and use all their fantastic machinery to capture us. I expected to be nearly caught by now. But although in the beginning there were voices that seemed close enough on our tracks, suddenly they stopped. Behind us we could hear shouts. Men shouting, women shouting, children shouting. It was mad. The farm was always so orderly, so quiet, so peaceful. And suddenly everything collapsed into complete mayhem. I wondered what was going on. Maybe that was it - mayhem. Everyone was rioting. Maybe they did it for us, maybe it was just bound to happen sometime anyway. But clearly those men who were chasing us initially, were not running after us any further.

In my mind, though, I did not fool myself. The White Suits had all the capacity to catch us later if they so wished. They had machines. They had power. They had authority. They could reach any place inside the Farm – and outside of it. There was a folk story doing the rounds on the Farm, about a girl of fourteen seasons who tried to run away once. Some said her name was Lilac, others insisted her name was Michaela. Whatever her name was, I'm not sure why, but she ran away and no one had seen her for days and days. White Suits finally found her and returned her. They saw a White Suit carrying her body so the assumption was that she got herself injured. The White Suits took Lilac or Michaela to The Shed and she never came back out. We could only speculate on the events that were unfolding behind us. Our faces were looking ahead, not back. We kept running.

11 THE FIELDS

We reached the wheat fields. The wheat was tall and gently scraped my face as I ran through. Every year when time came to plough these fields the White Suits came with gigantic ploughing machines. We all helped gather the wheat. We kept what we needed and the rest was taken by the White Suits. The same happened with the corn. It was one of my favorite chores. I loved the smell of freshly ploughed wheat. The work was hard and backbreaking at times, but I did not mind it. I loved the long afternoons in the field, the late sun, the kind wind on my face. It never occurred to me that one day I would be running for my life through these fields, trying to reach far beyond them, into the unknown.

It was difficult to keep running hand in hand so I had to let go of Snotty's hand. But now that she was not physically attached to me, a new fear sneaked into my mind that I would find myself at the edge of the wheat field, about to run into the corn, and would not find her. That she might fall behind and be taken. Suddenly her presence there with us was immensely reassuring for me. I don't know how to explain it. It wasn't only that I was grateful to her for saving us the way she did, locking the door on The Shed behind us, but I was also just genuinely happy she was there. I wanted to call to her. To make sure she was running beside me. I wanted to call to Rosichi to make sure she was there too. But I didn't. It wasn't exactly that we kept to stealth mode; we were breathing hard, our feet pounding the ground as we ran. But still, I didn't want to make a vocal sound; I didn't want the slightest chance of being heard back at the Farm, even though the distance by then was far too great for that to happen.

I had run this way many times before, but never this fast, never this urgently, never with this much dread. Wheat kernels and dust blew into my open mouth and made me cough. I used to run here laughing, my hands spread at my sides, feeling the wheat, letting it caress me gently. This time its resistance against my body was aggressive and unkind.

Finally, my body bolted out of the wheat field and onto the dirt road that stretched unevenly between the wheat field and the corn field. I stopped briefly to catch my breath. I was pretty sure I was the first out and needed to ensure Snotty and Rosichi were close. I still did not want to call to them. I didn't want to give our pursuers the slightest hint as to our whereabouts.

Surprisingly, next to run out of the wheat field was Snotty. She stopped in her tracks.

"Are you OK Sunny?" she asked, panting hard.

"Yeah... Just wanted to make sure you two were behind me... Keep running. Don't stop until you get to the pond," I said, barely able to steady my own voice. Snotty nodded and without hesitation disappeared into the corn. The tall crops parted ever so slightly to allow her through and then closed behind her, as if they were in on her secret.

Everyone knew the pond and how to get there, but I don't think anyone visited the pond as frequently as I did.

Time was ticking. It was probably only a few seconds but in our panicked haste, it seemed like hours. Fear started to grip my stomach. Rosichi was always so light on her feet. Petite in build, she was always the best runner of us all. Maybe she had outrun me? Maybe she was already ahead and I was still wasting precious time here? I was getting nervous. Do I stay and wait? Do I keep on running?

I decided to count to ten and then start running again. I counted slowly, dragging the count just to be sure. I think it was at about eight that Rosichi managed to stumble out of the wheat. She was flushed and breathing very hard. She noticed me and stopped, bending over, her hands on her knees, trying to catch her breath.

"Rosichi, are you OK?" I asked her. But I was deeply concerned. This was very unlike her. It should have been me going all red and breathless. Something was off.

I got to her and touched her shoulder. "Are you all right?"

She didn't answer. She was still fighting to breathe. She nodded.

"Is it the wheat?" I asked, although I knew it couldn't be. Rosichi was never allergic to wheat before. Other girls could not get anywhere near it without sneezing for hours and grasping for air. Rosichi was never one of those.

"No," she panted. "It's OK. I'm OK. I'm fine." She rose up. "Let's keep going."

I nodded, still suspicious. I let her go into the corn field first and entered right behind her.

I was no longer short of breath but instead I felt heavy with worry. Rosichi kept stumbling ahead of me, just barely avoiding a complete fall to the ground. It was like her legs were weak and confused. I didn't know how to help her. My only thought was to keep going. I was hoping she would get better.

The corn field was vast. It took us a while to reach the pond. Snotty was there waiting.

Rosichi sat herself on the ground.

"Sorry. I'm holding you back," she said, breathing hard.

"What's wrong Rosichi? I asked her.

"Nothing. I'm fine," she responded, avoiding my eyes.

Snotty looked at me, question marks in her eyes.

"You are not fine," I said quietly. "You are not yourself".

There was silence. Heavy and sticky silence. Snotty and I were looking at Rosichi. Waiting.

Rosichi's hands reached to the ground and slowly she raised herself up. She looked at us, lifting just a little the edges of her tunic.

My heart fell. An involuntary gasp escaped me. I put my hand to my mouth.

On the sides of Rosichi's inner thighs there was blood. Mostly dry and smudged, but I knew. I knew then. What happened to Dawn, they did it to Rosichi too. And I didn't mean to but tears started rolling out of my eyes.

Rosichi started to weep.

"It hurts," she said.

Tears streamed down my cheeks. I cried with her. "I'm sorry." I whispered. "I'm so sorry."

I should have made an effort to get to her earlier. I should have run to her the first time she called my name in that darned room. Why did I wait? Why did I hesitate?

"I should have found you," I said, "much sooner."

"It isn't your fault, Sunny!" she said, and her voice was all of a

85

sudden so full of anger. "Not everything is your damn fault! Not everything is your responsibility! Stop pretending to be my mother all the time!"

I didn't expect that. It completely bowled me over. I said nothing. A sense of total confusion hit me again. I felt like I was losing my compass, not knowing what to do next and why things were happening the way they were. Not knowing what to expect or what to say. I was losing the little perceived control on my life I had left, deprived of all apparent logic, stripped of all ability to make sense of my existence. It was terrifying.

"I'm sorry…" Rosichi said quietly. "I'm sorry. I didn't mean to say that. I don't know why I said it… I don't even feel like that! You are my best friend… I don't know why I said it."

She got closer to me and took my hand. She looked at me with her teary sad eyes. There was sincerity in that look. And deep pain.

I nodded. I didn't feel like there was anything to forgive, to be honest. I still felt like I should have done a better job at this running away thing.

Snotty gave Rosichi a quick hug. "We must keep going," she said. "Everyone will assume we are at the pond. We can't stay here."

She was right. How come this seven seasons old girl kept being right all the time?

But truth was, I had never wandered past the pond. None of us had.

The pond was far enough as it was; it was the unspoken boundary of our existence. Any step we took beyond this point would be the first we had ever taken. I didn't know how much further the corn field stretched, or what lay beyond it.

"Can you keep running, Rosichi?" I asked her.

"Yes, for now," she said.

I looked at Snotty. "Rosichi goes first, then you, then me." Snotty nodded.

"We keep moving north," I added. "There," and I indicated with my hand where we should be going. I knew we needed to keep heading north, and north is normally the direction from which the wind blew. I had spent so many hours giving my face to the wind that it filled me with a quiet confidence that as long as we followed the wind's direction we would not be walking in circles.

Rosichi wiped her hands on her tunic and started running, Snotty behind her. I joined them at the back, closing the ranks of our sad little herd.

12 CRACKS IN THE ESCAPE PLAN

I'm not sure how long we kept running, but after a while it was clear that Rosichi could not maintain a fast pace. She just abruptly stopped. Snotty was too late to notice and ran straight into her. Rosichi fell to the ground with a thud. It brought to my mind the night we went looking for her mom. That night was the black shadow that had fed my nightmares until now. But ever since that morning there had been new material for nightmares. Far darker, far more sinister.

Rosichi gave a short whimper and rolled over on her side.

"I'm sorry! I'm sorry!" Snotty kept saying sweetly. Seeing Rosichi so frail, so easily floored gave both of us quite the fright.

Rosichi did not respond.

"Maybe we should stop for a while?" I suggested.

Snotty seemed alarmed. "But we haven't gone far enough!" she said, her childish voice high pitched.

I sighed. I agreed with her. It worried me a great deal that we hadn't gone far enough.

"Can you stand up Rosichi?" I asked her softly. I leaned down and patted her shoulder as tenderly as I could.

She blew her nose loudly and sighed. For a while she just lay there, but then suddenly made an effort to pull herself up again. She was a bit wobbly on her feet, but she was up.

Worry really ate at me. We will not get far with Rosichi in this condition.

"Snotty, you go first," I said to her.

"Can you walk unsupported, Rosichi? You could lean on me," I said.

She gave a faint smile. "I can walk," she said, and followed Snotty.

The pace was slow. The corn field stretched on and on. This was new territory, but all we saw was corn. Further and further the field stretched. Or maybe it only seemed so to us, due to the very limited progress we were making.

Walking behind her, I observed Rosichi like a hawk, prepared to catch her when she fell. I noticed she was holding her lower abdomen with her right hand. It made me cringe with sorrow. She was so girlish, so fragile looking, so fair and so undeserving of such brutality. I wanted to hug her, but I just kept walking behind her in silence.

It was obvious that we would not be out of the corn field before nightfall. The sky was going dark around us.

I suggested we camp for the night where we were, when suddenly I could clearly hear the familiar sound of the Sky Noise. Those Sky Noise objects kept appearing out of the blue, and disappearing as suddenly as they appeared. This one hovered above us for a long time. I was filled with dread. Was that how the White Suits kept track of us? It made sense. They called off the chase because they knew where we were, and sooner or later they would intercept us and take us back to The Shed. They would strap me to the chair, they would push things into me…

The Sky Noise remained static over us. A menacing black cube, stabilized with small wings, and several metallic antennae protruding its top and sides. I looked at it. What will they do to us? Can they shoot us through that thing? Can they inject us with syringes with it? What did it do for them? My heart was pounding.

"Hey!" I shouted up at the Sky Noise, waving my hands like mad. "Hey! What are you going to do to us? Huh? What?"

The Sky Noise did not move. Nothing happened. It just kept hovering above us with its loud motor. I could swear, it looked back at me. There was an eye. A black eye that moved here and there, and it was fixed on me.

I looked over on the ground, trying to find stones to throw at it. I was not a great thrower, as the incident by the women's dorms proved to me the night we went looking for Rosichi's mom. But the Sky Noise was drilling into my senses with its impending presence, I had to fight it somehow.

I picked a stone and threw it hard into the sky. I missed the Sky Noise, but the eye – it moved. It followed the stone.

I was enraged. "Where are you? Why are you playing with us?"

I searched for another stone. Snotty was quick to join in. "Here, try this one," she said, handing me a decent size rock. I used all of my contempt for the White Suits to power my throw. This one came very, very close to hitting the Sky Noise. But I missed.

The black eye watched me. It was almost bulging out of its socket. But the Sky Noise did not move an inch.

It wouldn't go. I couldn't hit it. They will come soon, it was only a matter of time.

13 SNOTTY'S STORY

Given the circumstances, having been spotted by the Sky Noise, with Rosichi barely able to keep walking and the night falling fast around us, there was no point going on. We all agreed to stay put until sunrise. That is, unless the White Suits cornered us sooner.

Rosichi dropped to the floor like a marionette set loose from her wires. She cradled herself and closed her eyes.

It was not a very comfortable spot. We had to squash and flatten several corn stalks to be able to lay down, but I suppose it was as good as any spot in the field.

The Sky Noise kept hovering above us until it suddenly disappeared and silence befell us. Light wind whooshed softly. In my mind I was preparing myself for the inevitable ambush.

I laid on my side facing Snotty. It was now completely dark. Crickets were chirping happily. I couldn't sleep.

"Are you awake Sunny?" Snotty whispered.

"Yes".

But she said nothing more.

I wanted to ask her how come she was at the back door. I was curious to hear her story, but right then, all I wanted is to enjoy the silence and just sink into it whole.

I opened my eyes abruptly. Light was only faintly brushed across the skies. The world was at the verge of awakening to a new day.

I was still on my side, on the ground, in the corn field. My arms were aching.

I must have fallen asleep after all, against the odds.

Snotty was asleep next to me and Rosichi behind her.

We were not grabbed in the middle off the night by lurking White Suits. No one came for us. There were no more Sky Noise objects in the sky watching us. Only the wind and the corn and the crickets and us.

My throat was parched. I realized that I hadn't a drop of water the entire day. With the shock, and the fear, and all the running, it hadn't bothered me before quite as much as it did that very moment. But then, all of a sudden, it was the *only* thing that bothered me. We *had* to get to water.

I touched Snotty gently and she jumped up. "Is it morning?" she asked.

"It is," I said.

She rubbed her face and her hair. "Sunny, I am awfully thirsty," she said.

"I know. So am I. But we can't do much about it right now. We must find the edge of the farm. Hopefully we'll come by some water on our way."

"And then what?" she asked.

And then what…? I didn't know. In my mind I was hoping for a gate, open wide, or a hole in the fence. I had no clue what we would do once we got to the edge of the farm or how we might mitigate the fence issue, the fence that had the ability to repay you with death for the slightest touch. I knew that my focus must remain on putting as much ground as possible between us and The Shed. I hadn't considered the rest of it. I had never been asked to do anything like this before. So far it seemed, I wasn't very good at it.

"I'm not sure, Snotty," I said frankly. "We'll have to wait and see."

We woke Rosichi up. She felt cold to the touch. Her eyes were puffy.

She sat up slowly.

I almost could not recognize her. My witty, quick thinking, energetic friend was gone. Instead was a girl that carried the sadness of the world and all of its pain, inside her. She had that faint air of resentment around her again. I decided not to fuss and provided her with some space, even though it unnerved me to notice that some fresh blood has trickled onto her tunic during the night.

I stretched my neck and offered my face to the wind, assessing where north was. We started marching, picking up the pace but not running.

Somehow my spirit was slightly lifted. I don't know why, it was completely illogical to feel even a tad happier when the world was still in such turmoil around us, when nothing was certain and we had no idea where we were going. And still, I sensed a tickle of ridiculous hope.

The sun was rising. On and on the cornfield stretched. Thirst was becoming a real problem. I was getting dizzy. Rosichi stumbled several times but managed to get herself up unaided. I started to think the world must be completely made of cornfields, endless cornfields stretching further to eternity. The faint tickle of hope that had awoken inside me at dawn was all but gone by noon. We were destined to die here, dehydrated and clueless, covered with corn.

But then, just as unexpectedly, the last of the cornfield's rows closed behind us and we found ourselves standing in a field. A vast carpet of deep green grass welcomed us, dotted so wonderfully with colorful wildflowers. This was such a profound contrast with the dreariness of the living compound, the vile green of The Shed and the simple uniformity of the cornfield that I sensed even Rosichi's spirit had lifted at this delightful sight. The fields stretched far into the distance, where small trees decorated the horizon.

I felt like running wild into the grass and rolling eagerly in the glorious lushness. Instead I just stood there, on the verge of all this delight, looking up, and waiting for the Sky Noise to detect us. On this carpet of beauty we were completely exposed. I watched and waited. And waited. And waited. There was no Sky Noise to be seen or heard. Nothing but the lazy sun and a selection of fluffy clouds awaited. There was nothing to do but keep going. Unceremoniously we just marched on.

I may have even smiled initially, as we were walking through the field. I noticed every flower, every bee and every beetle. Snotty giggled when an orange butterfly fluttered around her hair. She skipped for a while. Even Rosichi quickened her pace. But after what seems like an hour or two the novelty of our new scenery wore off and thirst and despair returned in earnest.

It seemed like we walked for hours and hours, yet the trees on the horizon remained small and out of reach.

We walked in silence, each absorbed in her own little world until suddenly out of the blue Rosichi said "Why are we here?"

I didn't answer. I was a little confused by the question.

"We're escaping," Snotty answered, a tone of surprise to her voice.

"Yes. But why are we *here*? On the farm? Why are we here at all? Who made us? Why? Why were we born here?"

I didn't know what to say to that. I didn't know the answer. There were things that were bigger than us. Beyond our comprehension.

"Have you ever wondered why our moms allowed this to happen, Sunny? I mean, the great and powerful Stella… and what? Had all her boys dead and floating in a jar! And allowed you - her daughter! - to be… to be… to be…. ripped open and… and… used…. and used against her will!" Her voice broke.

"What does she mean, Sunny? 'Her boys dead and floating in a jar'?" Snotty asked.

"It's nothing," I said. I was really not going to get into that conversation. It was preposterous. My mom did not want me to get hurt. It wasn't possible.

"It is *not* nothing, Sunny!" Rosichi growled angrily. She was getting really worked up. "Your mom sent you to The Shed even though *I* was trying to help you stay out of it by lying for you! What kind of a mother does that? And she knew! I mean, she must have known! Isn't that exactly what they did to her? And to my mom? And everyone's mom? Your mom too Snotty. Why did they allow it to happen? To them? And to us? What kind of people do that, Sunny? They abandoned us! They abandoned us to the evil people…"

I was about to respond when Snotty cut in. "That's not true! Stella did not abandon Sunny!"

I looked at her, eyebrows raised. It was definitely time we heard her story.

As we kept walking on, Snotty began talking.

"After you left the community room I followed you," Snotty said.

I chuckled. She always followed me around, this girl.

"I wasn't planning to go into The Shed but I thought I might catch a glimpse of what was going on in there and what you were all doing… So, I came closer, but not too close…. I didn't want the White Suits to take me in there or anything… So, I started walking around to the Sick Room to see if maybe you were taken there or something… but the Sick Room's door was shut and there was no one outside at all… you know how normally there are the Patrol Women, but they weren't there. No one was. Which was strange, I thought. So, I just waited not too far from the graves. I just stood there, you know, not doing anything… it wasn't like I was *sleuthing*..."

The way she said it, it was pretty clear that this was exactly what she *was* doing… sleuthing.

"When your mom caught up with me. She grabbed me from the back and made me totally jump. I nearly died from fright. She was quite…" Snotty was searching for the right word, "disturbed, I guess… No, hysterical."

"How do you mean… hysterical?" I asked her. My mom was never hysterical. That didn't sound like her at all. She was always in such command of herself, and everyone else.

"It's the way she was talking. It didn't make much sense," Snotty explained. "She asked me if you went into The Shed... maybe five times she asked it... and I got a bit confused because I thought she was the one who sent you there..."

"She didn't send me there. She sent me to the Sick Room, to get Rosichi," I said. I didn't like how my mom was facing a field trial today with my friends. "I went after Rosichi."

"You know it's funny... you went after Rosichi and I went after you and your mom went after me... Funny eh?"

It wasn't, really. I thought it was a bit annoying how Snotty was finding this whole thing amusing. But I knew she was just young. To her, everything was one big adventure.

"Anyway, she was walking here and there and rubbing her forehead like..." Snotty gave an impression of my mom being worried, rubbing her forehead with her hand. "And she kept saying 'No, no, no, no, no, this isn't happening' and so on. Then suddenly, she took my arm and walked me with her around the Sick Room towards the west corner... you know... the White Suits' entrance!... I was getting a bit scared but she was walking really really fast!" Snotty was getting very excited. "There were several of those white vans that are often parked outside there.... You know the White Suits' vans. So, we ran and ducked behind one of those. The vans were empty, but I didn't know that until *after* we were already there..." she chuckled. "I thought we were done for."

"Then what?" I asked.

"We just waited. We waited and waited and watched the entrance for a long time. Nothing was happening. Until suddenly a White Suit came outside, through that door. We hid behind the van. I thought he would see us. But he was just standing there smoking. I swear Sunny, he had some blood on his suit. I was scared. But your mom was holding my arm and she just put her finger on her lips."

Yes, that has always been my mom's way of hushing me.

"The man went back inside. He stood in the doorway and threw the cigarette on the ground behind him as he was walking in, but the door, he didn't shut it, and the lock was left hanging loose outside… I *bet* they are going to send him away now!" she giggled. That idea of the White Suit getting into trouble amused her no end. I admit, it amused me too.

"Your mom then just started talking to me, really, really fast. She was going on and on about making sure that as soon as you are out, you must run away. Run far far away. Beyond the trees."

"Beyond the trees?" I asked suddenly in surprise. That was new.

"The orchard?" Rosichi asked.

"No. 'The trees,' that's what she said."

"Those trees?" I asked, my finger pointing ahead of us where the trees on the horizon now grew from the size of mushrooms to the size of small bushes.

"I don't know... she wasn't specific. But she said it over and over. Find you. Tell you. Run far away. Beyond the trees."

It was odd. The whole thing.

"Then we heard the commotion inside. People started running inside and shouting. Your mom left me there, and I got really curious... So, I sneaked out of my hiding spot behind the van and I got closer to the door. Honestly, I thought I'd only peek in, just to see what was going on, when I saw you two running like crazy. Then I grabbed the door and I decided to close it behind you."

"You saved us," Rosichi said. Snotty smiled proudly.

Something didn't quite add up. Why wasn't my mom still there?

"My mom *left* you there? Where did she go?" I asked.

"She said she was going to buy you some time. She was going to give them something to do," Snotty chuckled.

"What do you mean?"

"Stella went to set the women's dorms on fire."

14 TO THE TREES

So that's why they didn't follow us. They were preoccupied with the fire my mom started.

I felt so proud, and yet, remorseful. I never truly doubted my mom, but I should have given her more credit. She did not abandon me. All the time she was watching me.

I missed her.

We kept walking in silence. Thirst was constantly troubling me. The more I tried to put thirst out of my mind, the more it bothered me. It was now a rough, little, feral monster clawing its way deeper and deeper into my throat, clouding my thoughts and my vision and my mind, adding weight to my feet.

I didn't know how long we could last. Surely not much further before we couldn't go on.

I was watching my steps, looking to the ground, making sure to keep putting one foot after the other, when I raised my eyes after what seemed as a long time of constantly fighting off thoughts of deepening dehydration, I could see the trees. They were much closer now. They actually looked like trees. And I could clearly make out the fence line in the horizon, too. The hissing beast stretched from side to side all the way across the horizon and through the trees.

Mom told Snotty to go beyond the trees, so first we needed to get *to* them, so we could go *beyond* them.

I turned my head back towards the cornfields. I don't know why, I just wanted to get some measure of how far we already gone. Not that I trusted my dried-up senses by then, but I had a feeling that knowing we had already walked a great distance, would motivate me to continue pushing on. I was relieved to realize that we did indeed cover a lot of ground. The cornfield was now small and faded.

I thought I saw something else there too. I stopped and focused my eyes. It was still there. The Sky Noise. Just where it was the day before, hovering in a spot above the cornfield. I kept walking but it bothered me, so I stopped and looked again. Snotty stopped as well.

"Is that a Sky Noise over the cornfield?" she asked.

"I think so…"

It made little sense though. Why would it be there, when we are here? Completely exposed out in the open? If the White Suits were tracking us from afar, why would they not be sending the Sky Noise to follow us?

I had no answers. Just one more unresolved oddity to add to the ever-growing pile of riddles hanging above us.

We kept walking. Catching up to Rosichi was not difficult, as she was slow. I fully expected her to drop down from exhaustion any time, and rather soon. Instead she did something I totally was not expecting. She started chatting.

"Remember when we were kids, Sunny? Remember how we used to hide spiders in Flower's bedroom? She went into a fit every single time. She only discovered it was us months later and told on us to my mom." She giggled, "And remember... my mom suggested to her that we may have done it because we were taught spiders are drawn to pretty little flowers, and that perhaps it was a compliment not a prank... oh sweet Mercy... that was so funny... and Flower came to thank us for our kindness!... We couldn't stop laughing afterwards... Remember?

I chuckled. "Yeah."

"She started collecting spiders herself afterwards," Rosichi laughed.

I had to giggle. "We were a bit mean though..."

"I know... But we were so... brazen... Fearless..."

"You still are!" Snotty interrupted. I fluffed her hair. The way my mom used to do to me. It sent a shiver down my spine, the memory.

"We were happy," Rosichi said.

Yes, we were. Our childhood was rather blissful at the farm, yet it hid so much evil and pain; as children we did not see it. We were completely unaware of the amount of suffering our mothers had to endure because they endured it in complete silence. The vision of Freckles and Alberta and all the other women in The Shed flickered through my mind again. They were out of it. Sedated or drugged or injected with that thing they gave Dawn. Their eyes were not focused, they were oblivious to their surroundings. They must have spent hours… years… going through this pain. Hurt, undignified, having babies, seeing them die… and then being sucked from their breast. And all this time we were playing and learning things and pranking our friends. Ignorant of the bigger picture. We never, not once, asked who the White Suits were and why they were there. We just accepted their presence. They were part of our world, and we did not question our world.

For me, the world started changing the night I went to the Sick Room with Anne. The night I saw the floating babies. But I guess for my friends, oblivion endured, and their world only started changing with the appearance of the Sky Noises, and then the raid. Everything went askew after that. And since yesterday our entire happy bubble was burst forever. Even if we fell to the ground, debilitated with thirst and exhaustion, we could not go back. We could never return.

"I don't want to be a mommy," Rosichi just blurted out. "I don't. No one asked me. And even if they asked me I would have said no."

I didn't know what to say to that. The knowledge of what she was put through hurt. And I didn't know how to help her. How to ease her burden.

Rosichi went on, "You know those books at the community room…. They show you those colorful drawings of what the human body looks like and how babies are made. And in all those drawings there are always boys. Always dads…. involved. But there were no dads yesterday, only tubes and syringes and… humiliation!" she sighed. "Were the books lying to us, Sunny? I really need to know. Why would the books lie?"

I bit my lips. I didn't know why. I didn't think the books lied. I just thought what happened in The Shed was not right, somehow. An abomination of some kind. I kept my thoughts to myself though. Anything I might have said would only hurt her more.

The trees drew nearer and nearer. The closer they got, the quicker we marched to meet them. The fence grew with them too. It was the exact same fence that stretched by the dorms, formidable and massive, its thick skeleton separated by heavy poles every few meters, and the top pointing inwards almost flatly.

Here too, all along the fence, there was a road that stretched along its outside. Oddly, the road did not go through the trees like the fence, but around the entire section. We could not see the road beyond the trees, but it was visible again where the trees thinned and then disappeared.

The proximity to our initial destination filled us with delicate optimism. It seemed that we were going to make it!

The final few meters we nearly ran. The trees were thick and formidable and offered glorious shade. A tall tree was the first to greet us. Its long branches stretched as if to shake our hands. I put my hand on its flaky bark, sort of hugging it. In a weird way it felt like an ally. A friend. Someone who was waiting for us, conspiring to offer us discreet and cool hiding. Deeper into the trees we went, inhaling the calming earthy scent all around us. We were now completely surrounded with trees. But there was no elated satisfaction. There was no joy. Because still, we did not know where to from here, or how on earth we were supposed to get out.

"So now what?" Rosichi said it first. "What else did Stella want us to do? Fell the trees? Jump the fence? Die of exhaustion?... Because we are about to."

"I don't know," I sighed. Why did they always think I held all the answers? "But we should probably find the fence."

Amongst the trees it was not only cool and shady but a little darker. It was like entering a fantasy world, existing in its own right, undisturbed. If someone had told me that elves and pixies lived within these branches I would have believed it. The fence divided the trees into two parts, and it seemed that the part that stretched on the other side of the fence was even denser than the part we were fenced in.

Here, the fence seemed even more alien and out of place. The general darkness of the woods made it look even more sinister than usual. We were nearly at the fence now, when two incredible things caught my eye and could not have been avoided. The first was a sort of gap in the fence. Well, not exactly a gap, the fence was still there, but there was something covering a small patch of it. It looked like a plastic of sorts. A tarpaulin sheet possibly. It was so bizarre that I was almost tempted to try and touch it before I remembered the fence was not to be touched.

The second incredible thing, folded and nicely laid on the ground near the covered patch of the fence, was something that only I would have been able to recognize and it made me skip a heartbeat.

"Sunny!" Rosichi called with a hint of excitement, grabbing my hand absentmindedly, "Isn't that your blankie over there? The one you had when we were little?"

Ok, so Rosichi was able to recognize it too. It was my old blankie.

*

I was my mom's first child. First pregnancy. Possibly, from what I now knew, her first time being in The Shed. She probably suffered the hand of brutality just like us, but I suppose she was a bit excited with having me after all, because during her pregnancy she knitted a beautiful blanket for me, made of bright synthetic fibers the color of the sunset. I loved that blanket. As a toddler "Blankie" was my loyal comforter. It went everywhere with me, even to the fields. Once I left it behind in the cornfield on ploughing season, which caused me such a great distress, mom was full of stories of how I screamed all that night, earning me the fury of some Patrol Women who forced a pacifier into my mouth, which I kept spitting out. It was probably the one and only night they allowed Mom to sleep in my room with me. It was an unheard-of concession. The next day Mom retrieved Blankie from the field. It was a bit worse for wear and I even found a little snail on it. The snail I kept in my room as it fascinated me, and Blankie returned to its loyal place by my side. I must have been nearly ten seasons old before Blankie became redundant in my life. Mom took it and kept it. I thought she saved it for Antim. Clearly not, as here it was.

*

But who put it there? What was it doing so neatly folded on the ground? I felt deep suspicion sneaking into my heart. Was it an ambush, aimed to lure us in? If so, it was very cleverly laid.

15 BLANKIE'S SECRET

I hesitated, but Rosichi and Snotty were already running to where Blankie awaited. I ran after them. Blankie was nicely folded. By the look of it, it had been there a while. A long while. Pale snails had taken hold of it, lazily digging holes in the fabric. It looked as if it had soaked up plenty of old rain and was blown dry by plenty of old wind, several times over. It had lost some of its cheerful brightness, but it was familiar and suddenly so comforting, as if it were nestled casually and safely on my warm and dry bed.

Even though I was still plagued with suspicion, I had to touch it. Confused, amazed, I squatted to the ground and touched it. The feel of the soft fabric was so recognizable, it was like touching childhood again. There was no question at all in my mind that this was indeed my very own friend Blankie and not an imposter. I picked it up in my hand. I was trying to be careful not to disturb the snails. I liked snails, and they liked Blankie so obviously we had something in common. But once Blankie was lifted off the ground we all gasped.

"Sweet Mercy!" Snotty said, her eyes wide open in wonderment.

Under Blankie, tucked together into the ground, were two large bottles of what seemed to be water.

We practically threw ourselves at them. I grabbed one and Rosichi grabbed the other.

"Hey…" Snotty complained, "What about me?"

"We'll share, don't worry," Rosichi said, fiddling with her bottle, trying to open it.

"Wait!" I suddenly had an unpleasant thought. "What if this is a White Suits' scam? What if these bottles were somehow poisoned?"

Rosichi unscrewed the top of her bottle and started drinking in huge gulps. "If I die, don't drink yours," she said, fervently guzzling water.

I waited only for another brief moment before I unscrewed my bottle and handed it to Snotty. "Here," I said. "Leave some for me eh?"

She took the bottle and drank in large gulps. I watched them both drink, my throat burning and dry. Rosichi took a break, wiping her mouth. She took in a deep breath, but then she kept drinking more. I let her. She was injured and traumatized. She needed to rehydrate more than I did. After a while Snotty handed me her bottle. The water was not even very cool, rather on the warm side, but it tasted so pure and so sweet and so wonderful. I'd never had quite so much appreciation for plain, warm water as I had in that moment.

A few moments later we were all sprawled on the ground. Both bottles nearly all empty. Our tummies were full of water, our limbs heavy, and suddenly there was this content that we found hard to contain. We leaned against the big tree near the fence and sighed. I took a bit of water in my left hand and tried to wipe the black ink off my arm. It smudged a little, some of it was marginally removed, but you could still see it. You could still make out what was written.

One One Five Seven Two. These numbers don't define me, I thought. I am Sunny.

"So… do you reckon your mom came here and hid it for us?" Snotty asked.

"For me and Sunny, you mean. Technically *you* were not supposed to be here," Rosichi said, teasingly.

Mom. I could see her in my mind, tall and strong, walking alone this entire distance, making sure to hide the bottles amongst the trees, away from potential discovery from the watchful road. It filled me with so much gratitude and love for her, I felt tears starting to form in the corner of my eyes. How brave and how daring must she be, to have come here and put these bottles in the ground for me, ensuring that I would find them by using Blankie as bait. I wasn't quite certain when she came here, but I had no doubt that she came here herself. I always knew mom cared for me but I never quite appreciated how deeply, and how diligently she was watching over me. How long was she planning this? My escape… I couldn't help thinking. Wondering.

When my eyes turned and my attention drifted towards the huge layer of tarpaulin sheet that completely covered the fence from top to bottom, both sides, making the flat part at the top seem like a neat bench. Suddenly I knew. And the knowledge shook me so deeply that I started crying, big salty tears streaming down my cheeks.

How she looked at him. How her thighs swayed from side to side in such a provocative way as she approached him. "*Hi. I'm Stella…,*" her voice so sugary sweet and so foreign. "*Hi. I'm Stella…*" I was embarrassed by her then, I didn't understand her, but she knew exactly what she was doing. That's what she was doing. Preparing my escape. She knew then. She planned this. This was why. My heart was pounding. I was bursting with love for my mom, for her bravery, her foresight. How blind I was, not knowing fully well that she would never abandon me to the White Suits, not without a fight. I rose up from where I was sitting and approached the fence.

"What are you doing?" Snotty asked, alarmed.

I knew exactly what was underneath that tarpaulin layer.

"What are you doing, Sunny?" Rosichi demanded now, anxiety in her voice.

I paid no attention to them. I just grabbed the plastic and pulled hard. I could hear Rosichi and Snotty screaming in the background "What are you doing?" but it was only a faint background noise. Loud and clear at the forefront of my mind, was my mom's sugary sweet voice echoing, "*Hi. I'm Stella…*"

The tarpaulin came tumbling to the ground. Underneath it a massive, thick blue rug covered the fence on both sides.

Rosichi and Snotty gasped. I just cried.

16 THE FENCE

Evening was starting to take its hold and darkness was growing, or so it seemed due to the general shadiness of the woods around us.

I was devising a way to climb the fence on top of the rug. We needed to make use of one of the solid branches of the big tree behind the fence. Some of its branches extended over the fence and towards us like stiff pointy fingers. I was quite confident that this was the reason mom chose this particular spot. The good-looking man must have really liked her a lot to come here, probably from the outside, I thought, and lay the rug just so, meticulously covering it with plastic against the elements.

"I'm a little too weak to climb," Rosichi said faintly. "Maybe we can camp here tonight and climb the fence tomorrow morning?"

That was absolutely out of the question. We had to escape as soon as possible.

"OK, I know how to do this" I said. "Snotty, you will go first. I will help you up on my shoulders. You get to the top of the fence, where it's nice and flat, and then tie Blankie to the branch. We can use Blankie and some help from you to lift ourselves up.

"She is too weak to be able to pull us up, even with Blankie" Rosichi said.

"I'm not!" Snotty said, defensively.

Hmm... maybe Rosichi was right. The last thing I needed was to have Snotty fall over the fence, breaking a leg or a hand or a neck.

"OK. You go first Rosichi," I started saying but she cut straight in. "*You* go first Sunny. You are both the tallest *and* the strongest. You can probably even climb this fence without any help at all. Get yourself up there and then you can help us".

I took a few steps back and ran towards the fence, jumping at the last moment as high as I could to get a hold of the fence and push myself up. It was a miserable attempt. I smacked my face onto the fence and slid straight back down. I tried again. This time I took several steps further back and ran to the fence. I made it slightly further, but climbing, it was certainly not.

"Oh, that's just dumb!" Snotty blurted angrily. "Are you trying to make her do this all night?" she said to Rosichi. "Here, I'm ready – put me up there."

I had to smile at her brashness. I lowered myself to the ground as much as possible while helping her climb up my shoulders. It took me a while to stabilize myself with her on top of me, but as soon as she felt comfortable enough she leaped effortlessly on top of the fence... nearly falling off to the other side, but grasping the branch and steadying herself very confidently.

I clapped my hands softly. "Nicely done, Snotty!"

She smiled.

She then did the thing I always wanted to do as a child, she bounced on the flat part and gave a small giggle. The fence responded with an angry hiss. Snotty froze and Rosichi and I took a step back.

"You shouldn't do that!" Rosichi said, "The fence might still fry you!"

Snotty balanced herself to keep very still, holding onto the branch for support. The fence gave her a deep fright.

We were all silent for a short time. The fence did not hiss again.

There was no time to lose. I threw Blankie up and Snotty caught it with one hand.

"You need to make a very strong knot Snotty," I instructed her.

"Don't worry" Snotty said, "Patrol Woman Anne taught me how to tie sweet peas to the climbers' frame. I'm pretty good at it."

I looked back at Rosichi with a little smile, eyebrows raised, mouthing voicelessly *"Patrol Woman Anne?"* We both had very different memories of Patrol Woman Anne than Snotty's. I realized then that Rosichi was not smiling back, and even though it was quite dark, she seemed very pale and remote.

"Hey, are you OK?" I asked.

Rosichi nodded very faintly.

"Are you still bleeding?" I asked.

She nodded.

I don't know what they did, but they messed her up big time. I was pretty sure bleeding continuously from your insides was not how it was supposed to happen.

"Hold on Rosichi," I said gently, "We are getting out of here!"

Snotty took some time tying blankie until she was happy. "It's ready!" she proclaimed and let it go loose towards us. I tugged and pulled but it held well. "That's a pretty good job," I said.

I turned to Rosichi, "You go first."

"You," she said. "I'd still prefer that you were the one to pull me up, not her."

I suddenly had that feeling. The dread. Metallic taste in my mouth. Something terribly bad was about to happen and I knew it with absolute confidence. A heavy cloud was ascending in my heart.

"Sunny?" Snotty's voice from above the ground sounded suddenly a little panicked, "There are lights far into the distance! I can see it from up here… they are moving fast!"

I knew it! They were coming.

"Please go first Rosichi!" I ordered her. But she refused. She didn't even attempt to grab hold of Blankie.

There was no point wasting time arguing. I grabbed Blankie and climbed the fence. Standing on top of the stretched flat part was surprisingly easy to do. I had to fight a deep desire inside myself to give it a little bounce. I always wanted to do that, but I knew that the fence would better not be challenged any further.

Now that I was up, I held to the branch and lowered Snotty gently down to the other side. To the beyond. She leaped the final distance to the ground. She was out. We did it!

I faced the inner side again, lowering blankie to Rosichi and getting ready to grab her hand as she climbed. Darkness was becoming very thick, but Rosichi was so pale, she was almost luminescent.

"Come on Rosichi! There is no time!" I said to her urgently, "Climb! Grab my hand!"

I could see the lights now myself, and I could hear them too. They were driving some kind of a field vehicle through the flower field. They were getting closer and closer very fast.

Rosichi only kept standing there, frustratingly non-responsive.

"Come on Rosichi!" I was getting a bit angry and a tad hysterical, "What's the matter with you?"

Rosichi turned her face around. The vehicle was very close now. Soon they would need to disembark and come through the trees on foot. They might be upon us in just a matter of a few short minutes.

"I am only slowing you down," Rosichi said suddenly. Her voice was very cold and flat.

"What are you doing, Rosichi?" I cried to her. Alarm bells were pounding so hard in my head it hurt. "Grab my hand! Grab my hand NOW!"

She did not grab my hand. Instead she walked a few steps further from the section of the fence where we were. She stood in front of the uncovered, unprotected fence, her voice could only barely be heard. "I can't go on, Sunny," she said. "I can't."

"Rosichi! Rosichi, what are you doing?" I was screaming now.

I could hear Snotty behind me crying, "Rosichi! Rosichi! No!"

Rosichi just stood there for a split second longer.

"I'm sorry," she said.

And then she touched the fence.

17 THE SHOCK

I screamed.

Rosichi's fair and delicate body was thrown in the air a few meters back and smashed forcefully against a tree. The fence shook so hard I lost my balance and fell off the top, still grabbing the branch. I jumped down next to Snotty and landed roughly, rolling over a couple of times. Snotty ran to me, crying. She raised me to my feet. I ran back to the fence. Rosichi's lifeless body was tossed on the ground, twisted. There was a smell... a smoky, burnt smell, very sweet and sickening.

Through the trees, four small glowing white rays of flashlights were clearly visible, coming fast towards the fence. There was nothing further to do. I had no time to release Blankie or to get back to Rosichi; we had to run. Snotty and I turned and ran as fast as we could as far as we could, in complete darkness. We reached a big tree with a wide and formidable frame that could hide us and dived behind it, our backs to the tree. I held Snotty in my arms, her head under my chin. We were both shaking.

The White Suits reached the fence.

"Check that one" a voice said. I recognized it immediately. It was the woman White Suit.

"She's dead," a man's voice answered. "Fried."

Snotty released a small, faint gasp. I squeezed my arms around her.

"Smells nice," said another voice, "Anyone got any seasoning on them?" There were snorts and chuckles.

I felt sick.

"Enough with that talk," the woman said angrily.

"Oh. C'mon. We're only kidding," the man said, and there were more chuckles.

"I said enough!" the woman commanded, her voice raised unpleasantly. No one chuckled further.

"Take this one to the Works," she said.

"She's useless," said a voice.

"Must I always repeat myself twice?" The woman sounded irritated and unamused. "Take her to the Works. She can still be processed. Do you know how much money we lose on every one of those things if we don't send them to processing? Tsk. And this one was still a juvenile. Not had a baby even once yet. No tits. No milk..." She sighed a bitter, vicious-sounding sigh. "What a waste."

We could hear movement, dragging of feet. Hauling and towing. I knew they were picking up Rosichi's gentle body and grabbing her. They were being rough, indifferent, like she was scum. Footsteps started fading in the distance but I dared not come out behind the tree. I felt that the woman was still there, still looking.

Suddenly a narrow beam of light was pointed into the trees beyond the fence. We could see the white light searching in the dark. Lingering on from tree to tree, illuminating the ground, branches and barks. The light came nearer and nearer to us, until it fell just next to us. She was pointing her flashlight directly at our tree. Snotty was shaking. My hand was on her head, my lips were pressed against her forehead. "Don't move," I whispered in her ear.

I was sure she would be climbing the fence any second. We'd left Blankie there, hanging and available. But it was pitch black now. There were no climbing sounds, no indication that she was jumping to grab Blankie or leaping over the fence. Instead she shouted into the darkness from behind the fence, "I know you are out there One One Five Seven Two! I will find you Girl! I WILL find you! DO YOU HEAR ME?"

She stayed there for a while longer, until I could hear her walking away. In the distance her voice was still loud and clear, venomously ordering the men, "Come back in the morning and take that stupid rug off the fence! We don't want any more of those girls getting silly ideas!"

We could hear the engine of the vehicle start and then fade away into the darkness. Silence returned. A faint, vile, smoky smell still lingered in the air.

They were gone.

Rosichi was gone.

I couldn't hold myself any more. I wept silently. Rosichi was gone.

Snotty and I kept hugging for a while. Then I released my hold and patted her hair and face. "They don't know you are here," I said. "They were only looking for me." That had to be a good start.

Snotty nodded.

"We must get away from here," I said. "Come."

18 BEYOND THE FENCE

It was pitch black in the wood. We walked slowly, feeling our way around with our hands, crushing leaves and being scratched by twigs. I was afraid we might be walking in a circle and straight into the fence. But that did not happen. Some instinct kept us walking straight north. As we came closer to the edge of the trees, the blinding darkness was lifted ever so slightly. I could see the dark skies stretched above us, a large white moon was shining peacefully, and millions of starts dotting the darkness like precious diamonds. They all made it much easier to see our surroundings, but except for the white gravel road, nothing was familiar.

We waited for a few moments before coming out of the trees. I was afraid to find a delegation of White Suits waiting for us on the road. I stretched my neck and watched the road left and right, left and right, as far as my eyes could see in the moonlight. There was no vehicle approaching, no flashlights dancing on the white gravel. They might be coming for us, but not tonight. Quickly we crossed the road and kept walking straight into the unfamiliar wilderness. Hand in hand and in silence. We were both in shock. The last few hours were not at all what I expected from our happy escape.

"Why did she do that?" Snotty whispered suddenly and I could hear the traces of tears in her voice.

"I don't know, Snotty," I said. "She was in a lot of pain... and she... I suppose... was feeling very sad about being hurt and used like she was. I mean, immensely hurt. Immensely used." I didn't know how to explain it exactly, I didn't have a word for what went on in The Shed. "She couldn't cope with it... it was too much for her."

"I wish she'd stayed," Snotty cried.

"I wish that very much too," I said. "But it was her choice not to."

I wiped my tears with my free hand. "We have to continue," I said. I could tell she was nodding.

My left ankle hurt from the fall I took and started giving me some real grief. The vile green rubber slippers I was wearing were ill-equipped for so much walking through wild terrain and were coming apart here and there, which made walking rather painful. But knowing what waited behind us made it all secondary. I bit my lips and pushed the pain out of my mind as best I could.

I could push the pain away but I couldn't push Rosichi out. The way she died. The smell. That whole day at The Shed. I was thinking about my mom, what she did for me, all the risk she took upon herself to facilitate my escape in this way. I was deeply worried about what might happen to her now. What might happen to Antim. I was thinking of Antim a lot. She was just a toddler. She might be happy right now as I was, but what would happen to her when her bleeding started? What would happen to her if my mom was no longer there to watch over her, like she watched over me? That thought really scared me.

I lost all perception of time. It could have been around midnight or it might have been early morning already. It was still very dark. I was almost sleep walking, so preoccupied and withdrawn into my thoughts as I was, I paid little notice to the world around us. Suddenly, a sound up above our heads penetrated my conscience. The noise that was now as familiar as it was malevolent.

"Sky Noise!" Snotty whispered.

There was no avoiding it. We had no shelter to hide under.

"Yes, they are onto us," I said. "But we must keep walking…. Let's make them work hard before they manage to take us back eh?" I was trying to sound confident and reassuring but to my own ears I sounded mostly pathetic.

The Sky Noise hovered above us for a good long while before it disappeared.

A burning thought bugged me. "We have to get that thing out of our hands."

"What thing?"

"We all have some sort of a machine, a transmitter of some kind, inside our bodies. Inside our arms. The White Suits can read it. It contains information about us."

Snotty gasped in terror.

"Yes, we didn't know either. We only found out when we were at The Shed," I said. "The White Suits have devices that can get all the data out of us. As long as the thing is inside our bodies they will be able to track us."

"What do we do?"

"I don't know… but we must remove it as soon as we can."

So far, the world outside the Farm was completely vacant. There were no people, no houses, no cars, no lights. No crickets even to serenade to the night. Just a light wind to soften our breathing.

"I'm tired," Snotty said.

"Yeah. Me too".

"When can we stop?"

"Not yet."

I was sure it had been hours. The first light of dawn started tinting the darkness. In this new light I could see that very far in the distance there was a little house. We still had a good few hours of walking ahead of us just to get to it. The more we kept walking, the further the house seemed to be getting.

I could feel Snotty next to me slowing down. Her arm became heavy. Walking under a rush of adrenaline is one thing, but now that we were just going nowhere, exhaustion caught up with her. She had only a very limited understanding of the horrors of the farm and The Shed, certainly not enough to keep her energy levels up. She was only a little child, I thought. I couldn't expect her to keep up with my pace.

Oh, what's the point, I thought. Sooner or later I would need to carry her on my back if I don't let her rest.

"Let's park here for a while," I said.

It was just bare ground. Nothing was growing on it but some weeds and thorns.

Snotty, who was clearly just waiting for me to give the cue, stopped in her tracks and laid herself down on the ground. I laid down next to her. She was breathing heavily and in seconds began to snore lightly.

I couldn't sleep. My thoughts were racing and I was worried that we were too easily spottable.

I turned over on my tummy. The tunic I was wearing was so thin and useless, I could feel every little stone on the ground pricking me. I raised myself on my elbows to take a better look. Morning light was now exposing all the small hills and all the crevices of the land. There was nothing growing, nothing built for miles. But there was definitely a small house in the far distance. I could also see now that there was a road ahead of us. A proper road, not like the dusty gravel one by the farm. It was black and sleek, and from afar I could see it shining in the sunlight. There was a big colorful sign by the road. It looked pretty. I could see some cars going in both directions. They seemed tiny, like little toy cars. Realization that these could be White Suits cars gripped me with fright. They must have been searching for us, I knew. I lowered my head down and let the sun warm my back.

Why are they looking for me? I thought. Why? Why can't they leave us alone? Why do I matter to them so much? The White Suit woman said that Rosichi was a waste of money. What money? I never had any money. I'm sure Mom never had any money either. We learned about money from books in the community room, but like we learned about so many other things in the world outside of the farm, we never actually seen any.

I turned to Snotty, just watching her, envious of her ability to shut down her fears and sleep. The little girl who always annoyed me by following me around everywhere, the girl I never bothered paying any attention to, had turned out to be not only very cute and outgoing, but also exceptionally brave. I patted her hair gently. Her face was quite dirty and had streaks of dry tears marking her cheeks. She was very peaceful. Her nose was button cute and it definitely was not snotty. I was trying to remember her real name but I couldn't. For as long as I could remember, everyone always called her Snotty.

It filled me with shame that I haven't even bothered asking her for her real name. The one her mother gave her. I wondered if she missed her mom. I never saw Snotty with her mom much. Unlike Freckles and Alberta, Snotty's mom wasn't close to Stella. I knew, vaguely, that Snotty used to have an older sister once, but her older sister died somehow. Instead she followed me everywhere like I was the replacement sister. When I came to think of it, I was not even sure why she followed me in particular. I was never very nice to her on the farm. I saw her mostly as a nuisance. But how lucky I was to have her there with me. I vowed to myself, from that moment on, to become the big sister she wanted me to be. I will watch over for her, I will look after her. I will love her as I loved Precious, as I love Antim.

I closed my eyes but I couldn't sleep. I just laid there.

"Thank you," I whispered.

Snotty kept sleeping.

Above us, again, the sound of the Sky Noise motor penetrated. I didn't even bother turning. I could feel its eye on me.

"Come and get me." I said. "Why don't you?"

19 THE LITTLE HOUSE

The sun was hot. I could hear cars on the road far away. I'm sure I heard the Sky Noise over us at least twice more, but there were no White Suits.

It was possibly afternoon when Snotty woke up from her deep slumber.

"Hey," I greeted her with a smile.

"Hey," she replied with her own.

"Feeling a little better?"

She yawned. "Yes," She stared at me for a while "but I'm really, really hungry."

I wasn't even once thinking of hunger until that very second she said it. And then all at once, my stomach shrank to the size of a raisin and I could feel very strong hunger pangs. In a flash I felt like I was famished. What wouldn't I give for a juicy apple right then. The thought made my mouth water.

I was contemplating whether to get up and start walking or wait for evening to come. But Snotty had to get up anyway to toilet herself so there was no point in lying around; we could just as well be walking towards that house.

The ground was yellow-orange and dry. The black road stretched ahead, however the further we walked, and as curves and hills became more obvious in the topography, I realized that we were on a higher-level plateau and therefore not as visible to passing cars as I feared. I could now see the pretty sign on the side of the road. I wanted to vomit. It was the Natures sign. "The REAL taste." Our path turned away from the road that disappeared from view. We were now facing the house directly and there were no further obstacles between us.

There was no fence around the house. We could basically just keep walking right in through the front door. A dusty road led to it from the back.

It was not a big house. It was all wooden and looked like it had known better days about a hundred years ago. Some of the roof tiles were missing, and some of the weather boards were falling apart. Why anyone would not look after their house and let it deteriorate like that, I wasn't sure. I never had a house just for myself, but I kept my little room at the Girls' dorms very clean and tidy. It was my little kingdom.

There was a large yard around the house, which had some very sad and faded grass attempting to grow on it, dotted with large dry patches. It was nothing like the lush green meadow we have walked through in the farm. There were some washing lines stretched on an umbrella-like stand, which was turning itself around in the light breeze. There was also a much smaller building to the side of the main house. It, too, was in a bad state.

"We should observe for a while before we are seen," I said. "It might be a White Suits house; it could be dangerous."

A large cart was laying at the yard, its wheels broken. It had some mud in. A few stubborn wildflowers insisted on claiming it. We ran the few last meters, squatting low, and hid behind the big cart. It smelled of dust and of fresh soil.

The house was not deserted. It had some open windows through which smells of cooking drifted which made me salivate hard. It also smelled of fresh soap and cleanliness, in complete contrast to the general condition of the house externally. I felt such a strong urge to just stand up, make myself seen, and walk in. I wanted so much for this seemingly simple place to be our haven. A place where we would be fed and washed, loved and cared for. Where we could stop running.

The front door opened in a crash. The door seemed to barely hang on its frame. A large, heavy woman came out heaving a large basked in her big hands. She was plain looking, older than my mom, but not an old woman. We moved behind the cart to better see her. Her back was to us. She laid the basket on the ground near the washing lines and was hanging out wet clothes to dry. One by one she picked up garment after garment and clipped it to the lines. The clothes were all quite large, and their colors were dull and faded, but they smelled of sweet soap. Around and around the lines the clothes went. Every time the woman bended towards the basket, her heavy chin met her large bosom and she let a faint groan escape. She was unaware of us watching her.

I wasn't sure what to do next, I was quite wary. Suddenly, Snotty's stomach gave a growl. It wasn't a huge growl but it was definitely audible. Snotty grasped her tummy, looking at me, terrified. She didn't mean for her stomach to growl, but she couldn't exactly control it. She was hungry. I bit my lips.

Although I was convinced that the woman heard it, she did not stop hanging clothes on the washing line. I suspected she was angling looks towards the cart but she didn't make any attempt to expose us. What was she planning to do? I couldn't be sure.

Another growl was suddenly audible, but it was not made by Snotty's stomach this time. It came from the dusty road. A car. A white car. It came up to the house, rumbling and raising a cloud of dust around it as it went. It stopped between the house and the smaller building. It kept rumbling and blowing dust, when the side door opened and out came the White Suit woman. I recognized her immediately by her short cut hair, with her sleek fringe neatly combed to the side of her forehead. She was wearing large shades. I gasped with fear. I signaled to Snotty to be quiet with my finger on my lips, the way Mom used to. We couldn't have her stomach growl again. But how she would be able to control it, I didn't know. Being hungry could very well be our doom.

The White Suit woman approached the large woman who stopped hanging clothes and was now wiping her big hands on the side of her blouse.

"Good day to you," said the White Suit woman, as she raised her shades from her eyes and placed them on top of her head.

The large woman only nodded. "Can I help you with somth'n?"

The White Suit woman seemed to be looking around, taking in the scenery. "Do you ever get strangers crossing your property Ma'am?"

"Strangers?" the big bosomed woman seemed to be confused. "Ya mean, like… thieves and dat sort of scum?"

The White Suit woman did not nod or make any confirmation sign. She just stood there, staring at the other woman.

"None crosses my property just like dat," the large woman said. "If they think'em takin' anything they're gonna be mighty sorry," she added. "Sure to Hell, I can shoot my goddam shotgun real good," she said and raised her heavy arm so it was level with her shoulder, making a gun shape with her finger and thumb and pointing it at the White Suit woman, quite menacingly. "I can shoot dem in the dark with me eyes closed and still blow their goddamn eyes out of dem sockets. I won awards for me shooting" she added proudly and lowered her arm.

There was an uncomfortable silence between the women for a moment. Finally, the White Suit woman said, "We are looking for a runaway Natures asset," the White Suit woman said. "Did you happen to shoot any runaways recently?"

"Don't know what you mean," the large woman said.

"A Natures girl. About fifteen years old. Big hair, copper-brown. Blue eyes."

"Run away from the farm, ya say?"

"Yes. Last night."

I held my breath. That was it. We were found.

"Already milking is she… your, uhm, asset?" asked the large woman.

"Not yet."

The large woman hesitated. "No. Never seen her."

I was quite surprised by that. I mean, I could swear that she knew we were there.

"Are you quite sure?" The White Suit woman took a step closer. "I would like to remind you that the asset is Natures' property."

"Are you standing on *my* property and suggestin' I'm lying to ya?" the large woman took a step forward as well.

The White Suit woman stood hesitantly. She stared at the other woman for a few seconds, then returned her shades to cover her eyes. She handed the large woman a card. "Please call this number immediately should the asset turn out to be on your property, Ma'am. Good day to you."

She went back to the car, slammed the door quite hard and disappeared in a cloud of dust.

The large woman observed the car for a few long moments, ripped the card into shreds and tossed into the basket. Then she turned towards the cart.

"Okay, you can come out now!" she said. "Those assholes are gone."

20 THE JESSOPS

We hesitated. Although the woman did not give us away, I wasn't sure if I should allow Snotty to come out. The White Suit woman only mentioned me, not her. Snotty was still an undetected fugitive. But it would not have been possible. Snotty was hungry and I would not leave her behind the cart.

"C'mon! Don't be shy there," the woman called.

Slowly and a little reluctantly we rose to our feet and came from behind the cart.

"Two of ya's!" the woman said with some surprise. "Arent'cha lucky that goddam bitch did not ask about this cute little one then?"

She looked at us for a long time, casting her eye on each of us from top to bottom.

"Well, you are a cute little one, aren'tcha?" she said to Snotty. "How old are ya?"

Snotty hesitated.

"Go on, you can tell old Thelma. I wouldn' bite'cha."

"Err... seven. I'm seven seasons old," Snotty said in a weak voice, fiddling with her fingers nervously behind her back.

The woman started laughing. Her laughter was a thunder of big rolling suctions, it was loud and a little over the top.

"Seasons!" She laughed, as if it was truly the funniest thing she had ever heard. Finally, she calmed down. "We aint' countin' breeding seasons out here girl," she still chuckled. "We count by years. If ya don't want dem assholes to get their hands on ya's you don't say no *seasons*, you get me?"

We nodded. I have never met someone who talked like she did. The language she used sounded almost foreign. Like we landed on the moon by mistake.

"And you're fifteen eh?" she turned her eyes to me. She looked at me, I mean really looked. I felt naked somehow.

"Well, well. Sweet Mercy," she said finally.

I couldn't decide what I thought of her, of the entire situation. She was so... different. I couldn't read her, I wasn't even sure I completely understood her.

"Well then, don't'cha just stand there, eh. Come inside. Thelma will feed ya's some dinner."

She turned towards the house and stood at the entrance. Her bosom left very little room to pass through, so she sort of inhaled and held it in, to allow us a little more space. Snotty walked first and I followed her close behind. As we stepped over the rickety porch and came through the door the woman, Thelma, shouted above my head in a manner that nearly deafened me "Uncle! We have company!"

Thelma moved behind us and closed the door. The inside of the house was wooden as well. Everything was wooden — the walls, the ceiling and the floors. It was old wood, some of it was rotten or eaten up, possibly by woodworm. It was a little messy but not too bad. There were some faded pictures on the walls, some old looking furniture. Nothing much.

"Wait here, my uncle would love to see ya's," she told us. "It ain't every day that we get such visitors," she said. Then she shouted into the house, "Uncle! Get your ass out here!"

From somewhere deep inside the house we could hear the screeching of furniture on the floor, followed by a sigh, then the shuffle of feet. Out into the corridor came a man. I had seen very few real men in my life. There were the White Suits, but I wouldn't qualify them as real men. They were like aliens to us. There were the workers, like the good-looking man who fixed things around the farm, but I never gave them much thought either. And there were the men in the posters of Natures, and in the books we had in the community room. They were not real either. This was a real man. And he was definitely the oldest person that I had ever seen, man or woman. He must have been a hundred years old. He was slim and not very tall. His head was half bald and half covered with grey hair, and the hair was thin and dull and a bit long on the sides. His face was very tanned and deeply creased. His lips were very thin and his chin very square. When he talked his teeth seemed to be a dark shade of yellow.

"Well, well, well… what have we here?" he said rather festively. He licked his lips with his tongue and gave a thin smile. "Sweet Mercy." He looked at us very carefully. "Natures girls eh?" He chuckled, "Sweet, sweet Mercy."

"This one is seven," Thelma said from behind us, putting her hand on Snotty's shoulder.

"Are ya, now?" the man said. "Why, aren't'cha a cute little button?" He chuckled again.

Then he looked at me. There was something about his look that made me shudder. I couldn't explain it. His look was not kind. He looked at me like I was at the same time absolutely nothing and entirely everything. "Well, aren't'cha the view for sore eyes," he said, smiling. He gave his lips another lick. "A fine specimen ya are, girl…. a *fine* specimen. Look at dem boobs on ya," he said, half to himself and half to Thelma. "Sweet Mercy."

I was still wearing my tunic, but I felt naked and embarrassed. I folded my hands together trying to cover my breasts. He looked at them so intently, it made me feel extremely uncomfortable. We should not have come here, I thought. These people were strange.

They made me feel wary... and very naked.

"Do ya have the sweet nectar coming out of dem boobs yet, girl?" he asked me, still with his very unpleasant smile.

I had no idea what he was talking about. Was he referring to the white stuff that came out of Alberta's breasts? Was that what we were supposed to produce for Natures? A sweet nectar of some kind...? With our breasts?

"Dat bitch woman said she ain't ready yet," Thelma said.

Her uncle only chuckled. His eyes still on my breasts.

"Well, did you have ya's bleedin' yet or no?" he sounded a little impatient.

"Uncle Jessop!" Thelma was growling at him like he was a naughty little child. "Don't'cha scare dem girls away, now. Leave dem alone. Look at dem poor things. Needin' to eat and to wash. Dat's no way of treatin' guests..."

Her uncle only chuckled some more; he finally peeled his eyes off my breasts. He turned around and went back inside the house.

I was glad to see the back of him, and I really just wanted to turn around and say 'Thanks, but we really have to go now,' but Thelma was a big woman and she was blocking the door. I was tired and hungry and so was Snotty. We had to let this situation play itself out a little longer.

Thelma pushed us gently through the corridor and pointed us at the stairs. "Come upstairs girls, Thelma will let ya's wash first. We don't want all dem filth at the dinner table now, do we?"

We climbed up the stairs. Snotty first, me following and Thelma behind us, holding the wooden rail to haul herself up, panting with every step.

The upstairs was wooden again, floor, walls and ceiling. It had a few small rooms and a decent sized bathroom. The bathroom was mostly clean. Thelma filled the bath with warm water and put some soap in. It smelled lovely.

"Go on, take ya's clothes off, Thelma will give dem a good wash," she said. She went outside the bathroom, and left the door wide open. Snotty and I looked at each other. It was so strange, but we both wanted to get the last 36 hours scrubbed off us. I took off my tunic. It was scratched and filthy. Snotty undressed hesitantly. I stood between the door and her young bare body. I needed to shield her from being watched. That uncle Jessop gave me the creeps. The thought of him watching us bathe was making me queasy.

We went into the warm water together, facing each other. It was lovely, so soothing and comforting. I rubbed the black ink off my arm. Gone was One One Five Seven Two. Snotty scrubbed her face, blowing bubbles into the water as she did. Her cheeks came out bright pink. Her tummy kept rumbling loudly, which made her giggle. I enjoyed her giggles. They were the giggles of a normal girl, having a normal bath, at the end of a normal carefree day. I really wanted to succumb to this feeling of normality. To this warm, perfumed bath. But I couldn't, because it wasn't normal. It was just the best that we could do under the very abnormal circumstances. Smells of cooking food drifted upstairs from the kitchen and the thought of a feed filled me with pleasant anticipation.

Thelma came back into the bathroom, holding towels and robes the color of faded peach, and a few other garments. She placed everything on the wooden chair in the corner by the basin. I made sure we were sufficiently covered with bubbles.

"Now, this one might be a little too big for ya darlin'," she said, looking at Snotty and pointing at one of the folded robes. "But it will take at least a day for ya's clothes to dry on the line. You will be fine with this one," she said to me patting the other robe that was on the top. "Now with dem shoes, you can't keep walkin' on these rubbish ones," she said, giving the vile green rubber slippers a little kick. "These are Thelma's old slippers," she said and put a pair of fluffy looking slippers down on the floor. They were the matching color of faded peach. It was all very... peachy. "Good on old Thelma for not throwin' those ones away eh?" She kept referring to herself in third person. I found that a little confusing and rather odd. "You can put ya's shoes back on," she said to Snotty. "Dem still in good condition. But I gave you a pair of socks here," and she picked up the pair of used-to-be white socks from the chair and waved them about.

We nodded and thanked her. To be honest, I was feeling very

grateful and more than a little unkind for being so suspicious towards Thelma's hospitality. So far, she was being very nice to us.

"Well now, don't'cha stay there too long, ya hear. Don't want dem wrinkles on ya's fingers and toes. Thelma will make ya's a nice dinner". She left the bathroom, the door wide open behind her.

I rose out of the water first and grabbed a towel. I wrapped it around me. It was a bit worn but it was soft and it smelled really nice. I grabbed the other towel in my hands and spread it open to fold Snotty's nakedness into it as soon as she raised out of the water. There will be no voyeurism with this girl as long as I am there to protect her.

I helped her dry and get dressed in the peach robe Thelma brought. It was indeed big for her, sweeping the floor at the bottom, but it wrapped around her completely, covering her nicely. I helped her into the socks and put her shoes back on. Then I dressed myself with the robe which fit me just right, I put the slippers on, they were a little wide but I managed.

Before we left the bathroom, I gave Snotty a hug. She put her hands around me and nestled her cheek on my towel. I wanted to cry suddenly. I was really fighting back tears.

"Snotty?" I asked her very quietly and softly, "What is your real name?"

She was quiet initially and then said in her small voice.

"It's Spirit."

21 AT THE DINNER TABLE

Such a beautiful name and I never even bothered asking her.

"I'm sorry for all the years I called you Snotty" I said.

"It's OK" she smiled up at me, "everyone calls me Snotty."

"Your name is beautiful. And it suits you," I smiled back, still fighting back those darn tears. "You are such a spirited little girl."

"Thanks," she said cheerfully.

I gave her another small fond squeeze and we left the bathroom and came down the stairs.

The staircase led back to the end of the corridor, which opened up to some sort of a sitting room. It had a large old looking wooden dresser with a few old plates on display, a faded picture on the wall with some creatures that I did not recognize, and an old looking small armchair. It was definitely too small to accommodate Thelma. We turned right into the living room. The lights were dim. We hesitated and took a brief look around. It was plain with a sofa and an armchair, both seemed to once have been burgundy-ish. There was a narrow coffee table with a white embroidered coffee table cover, stretched over the center. Uncle Jessop was napping on a rocking chair in the far corner. His head was tilted backwards and his mouth was open. His snores were quite loud. There was something very creepy about him, but in this chair, he looked harmless and a bit pathetic.

Thelma poked her head through the door. "Don't'cha mind that old bugger eh!" she said and chuckled very hard, as if reading my mind. I sort of started to like her a little. But I was still wary. "Come! Ya's can help Thelma set the old table."

We walked through the gap in the wall that perhaps used to have a door in it once, but now was just a space to walk through. We found ourselves in a dining room. It was all wood again, top to bottom. A heavy-looking wooden dining table stood in the center of the room. It looked solid but not very large. Four simple wooden chairs stood at the table, one per side.

"Uncle Jessop made it," Thelma said pointing at the table, "when he was young".

I found it impossible to picture Uncle Jessop as a young man.

A single pendant-style light with a peach shade hung above the table, casting a dim light. The shade had some fringes all around it and was hanging a little crookedly around the light bulb. Another heavy dresser was leaning against the dining room side wall. It was bigger than the one in the sitting room. It did not have plates on display but instead plates were stacked one on top of another. There were glasses and mugs positioned upside down on shelves and next to them a glass pitcher.

"Set the table for the four of us," Thelma said. "Ya'll find cutlery in the drawer."

Spirit and I set the table. No one plate matched another. They all had flowers and all sorts of pretty ornaments on them but each was different. We took forks and knives and set them nicely by the plates. There were at least two different sets.

"OK, Thelma will get the food on the table now," Thelma announced, then looked at me. "Girl, be a nice one, go get that uncle Jessop to the table eh? Wake him."

If she had asked me to go and smash my head against the wall I would have done it with more delight and willingness. Just the thought of having to stand near enough to that man, wake him no less, and get him to come to the table, made me extremely uneasy.

Slowly and hesitantly I went back into the living room where uncle Jessop was still on the rocking chair. He wasn't snoring. I had a nasty feeling that he wasn't exactly sleeping either.

"Uh... Mr Jessop?" I said, my voice quivering.

He didn't respond. Of course he didn't. I bet he was not sleeping. I bet he was enjoying this. I came closer.

"Mr Jessop?" I said, my voice a little louder this time.

No. Nothing. I had to get closer. I knew that was his game. I stood very close to him now.

"Mr Jessop?" I said and I touched his shoulder.

He opened his eyes and looked at me. He was smiling. It was not a nice smile.

"Mr Jessop eh?" he laughed a throaty laugh. "I ain't no Mr Jessop, girl. Uncle Jessop will do me fine," he said, and sat up a little in the rocking chair.

"Thelma asked me to get you to dinner," I said a little timidly. Gosh, I hated the way I sounded.

"She did now, did she?" he said and his voice drifted away a little. "She sent me a gift Thelma, eh?" he chuckled and without any hesitation he simply reached, grabbed my robe's tie and pulled it, opening my robe. As the one known for being able to smell danger a mile away I certainly did not see that one coming. I grabbed my robe and tried to cover myself. He laughed. He laughed so hard he was nearly choking on his own laughter. "What's the matter girl, getting all bashful on me now? We all know about ya's Natures girls, a bunch of teasing whores ya're, fucking dem suit boys all day. Think Uncle Jessop don't know?"

He sprang up from his chair and stood facing me, he was so close to me I could smell his sour breath on my face and it made me want to vomit. I felt my heart pounding so hard my veins were about to pop. I was still gripping my robe trying to hold it closed it when he shoved his cold, bony hand under it, and grabbed my left breast. He squeezed it very hard and kept squeezing and squeezing. It hurt me. I felt the tears were back. He just laughed. "I'ma gonna enjoy sucking that nectar out of ya girl! Oooh dem boobs on ya! Sweet Mercy." Then he just let me go and unceremoniously went into the dining room.

I stood there, ashamed, terrified and confused, and so small and insignificant. We had to get away from that sick place. That man was not any different from the White Suits, just grabbing our bodies, doing whatever they wanted with us. Thelma and all her sweet talking could not undo what just happened. I tied back my robe, this time with a double knot. I wiped the tears from my eyes and took a deep breath. We had to leave. Tonight.

I entered the dining room. Nasty Uncle Jessop was seated on one side of the table, Spirit next to him.

"Here ya go," Thelma pulled the chair on the far side from Jessop. I felt almost relieved, but also concerned for Spirit being the one closest to him. I sat myself on the chair and gave Spirit a look that was desperately trying to convey all my feelings. She may have understood, as her face clouded.

Thelma grabbed the plates we laid on the table a few moments earlier and returned them to the dining table one by one. "Here we go!" she said triumphantly.

Until a couple of minutes ago I was so hungry I thought I could eat a truckload of corn by myself. Now my hunger was gone.

Everything on the plate was coated with a thick brown gravy that was unrecognizable. It smelled nice though. Small cut carrots, several halved small potatoes and a mountain of peas looked very appetizing. The pendulum that moved between Thelma's attempts to spoil us and nasty Jessop's attempt to shame me was hard to manage. From gratitude to contempt and back to gratitude, in less than ten minutes, was more than I was used to handling. There was something else on the plate thought, something that looked different and smelled different. It looked like poop and reminded me those posters in the Sick Room at the Farm. The smell... it was sweet and smoky and sort of burnt at the same time, and it reminded me... it reminded me of the smell Rosichi left behind her when she touched the fence.

Thelma came back to the dining table with the last plate and sat herself down opposite Spirit.

Spirit was about to grab the fork when Thelma said, "We say our thanks first, Sweetie." Spirit took her hand off the table. She sneaked a side glance at me. I shrugged very lightly.

"Sweet Mercy, thank you for bringin' us today these two valuab... eh, precious... guests." She smiled at us. "OK ya's can eat now."

I tried to signal to Spirit not to eat the poop thing, but I realized she was not going to touch it anyway. She was a very perceptive child.

"So.... Natures girls eh?" Uncle Jessop started. He spoke while filling his mouth with the brown thing. It was vulgar.

"Uncle Jessop, please, not at the dinner table!"

"Dont'cha *Uncle Jessop* me Thelma!" he nearly shouted. "This is my goddamn house and I will say what I want wherever I want!"

Thelma went all quiet.

"Those goddam Natures assholes, I hate dem goddamn motherfuckers!"

Thelma was about to choke on her meal.

"Ya need to sell a kidney to be able to afford any of dem goddamn products. Peh. As if it was gold. Breeding dem bunch of whores they can fuck all day long, get the nectar going!"

He was talking and chewing, barely swallowing. His face reddened. "Keeping prices high so only dem rich boys can afford to enjoy their mommy's nectar, pushing money to all dem cocksuckers in the government...." He took a large bite of the poop-looking food. "Bloody bastards I tell ya, you call dat work? Surrounded all day long with all dat *pussy?*"

He said that with so much spite and rage, bits of food spat out of his mouth and flew everywhere.

Half of what he said I didn't understand at all. Obviously, he did not like Natures. I didn't like Natures either. One would have thought this could make us into allies, but the way he said it… the way he looked at me when he spoke. Something was off about the whole thing.

"Tried to get work in dat place once." He said half to himself, half to me, chewing his food with an open mouth, staring at me. "Turned me down if you'd believe it!" he pointed his fork at me, as if I had anything to do with his failure. "Those fuckers…. Emanuel Jessop not good enough for dem goddamn assholes eh?"

Thelma was moving in her seat with great displeasure "Uncle Jessop… please!" she was begging.

He paused for a brief moment.

"Did they put one in ya already, girl?" he said looking directly at me. "I bet they did, dem goddamn lucky fuckers! I bet ya liked dat one eh?"

I looked at him completely vacant. What was he asking?

"Well not you," he said to Spirit. Ya's too young eh… "ya'are…. eh… an investment."

Suddenly he started laughing, but all the food he was storing in his mouth did not agree with that and he started choking. I looked at him heaving and panicking, reaching with his hand to his throat, fighting to breathe, and something in me was extremely gleeful.

Sweet Mercy, I thought to myself, please make this the end of nasty Emanuel Jessop!

But Thelma jumped from her seat, which fell to the floor behind her, and smacked Jessop hard on his back. She could have broken his spine with that much force... but she didn't. Instead a piece of that poop-food came flying out of his mouth and landed smack down on Spirit's plate. She had already eaten most of her vegetables by then, thankfully. She didn't touch anything after that.

Jessop took a deep noisy breath in, and emptied his glass of water.

"Get to live another day," he said, and chuckled to himself.

"Sweet Mercy!" Thelma added. Then looking at Spirit's plate she immediately added. "Let me give ya a new plate girl, what would ya like?"

"Nothing, thanks," she said. "Everything was very nice but I'm full, thank you."

I knew she was lying. She was so hungry before, I'm sure she could have eaten more of the vegetables. They were actually very nice. I suppose her hunger disappeared with the company that we had.

"You ain't gonna eat dat?" Jessop said, and reached with his fork to the poop-food on Spirit's plate. "Dat's good for protein and iron girl, don't'cha know?" He grabbed it and loaded it onto his own plate. He chuckled and winked at Spirit. "Could be a relative, eh?"

I wished he'd stop already. I understood what he was insinuating. I remembered the talk after Rosichi's death. The picture of what was happening at the farm was becoming clearer and clearer to me. It made me dizzy and sad and sick to my stomach. Suddenly all the vegetables I ate threatened to come right back up again. I quickly took a sip of water and tried to calm my nerves.

We sat in silence, waiting for Jessop to finish eating everything on the table. He cleaned out all our plates, including Thelma's who was clearly quite upset about the entire show.

Finally, he finished, wiped his mouth, burped a small burp, and got up. He did not excuse himself or thank Thelma or anything, he just got up and left the dining room. I felt a little sorry for Thelma. She had to put up with him every day. It must have taken a lot of effort. And a good pair of ear plugs.

"Well!" Thelma said, trying to sound cheerful. "Shall I take ya's to ya's beds?"

22 NIGHT AT THE JESSOPS' HOUSE

The idea of sleeping in that house under the same roof with that vile man sent shivers down my spine. I planned to tell Spirit that we were leaving that very night, as soon as we were left alone in our room. We would sneak out after everyone was asleep, and we'd just run.

We climbed up the stairs after Thelma to the second floor. In front of us was the bath. I realized we left it in quite a mess and felt a pang of sadness, as the burden of cleaning would naturally fall on Thelma.

"Thelma, shall we clean the bathroom?" I asked.

"Oh, no… don'tcha mind the bathroom. I clean it every day. Thelma don't mind."

I thought she must have lived as a slave to her uncle. Domestic cleaner, cook and washer. No wonder she was happy to see us. In spite of the towels and the robes and the slippers and the lamp shades, it did not seem like her life was all that peachy.

She turned right and a few steps after we passed the bathroom, she opened the door to a small room. It was a small room, clean and tidy. A small wooden dresser that a long time ago was paint-brushed white stood by a medium-sized window. Long, pink curtains hung all the way to the floor, meeting a woolly pink rug at the foot of the small single bed.

A single bed.

It was nicely made with matching pink sheets and a pink duvet and a pillow. It looked very soft and comfortable, warm and inviting.

A single bed.

"There is only one bed," Spirit said, with note of worry in her voice.

"Oh yes, of course. D'ya like it? This used to be Thelma's room when I was just a little one like ya're." She patted the soft pillow "Nice and cozy."

"Where will Sunny sleep?"

"Oh, don't'cha worry little one, your friend is gonna sleep in the shed. We'll make it nice and cozy for her there too, don'tcha worry."

The shed.

I got scared. I could feel my knees buckling. "Where?"

"The shed. It's dat small shack just outside the door, next to the house. Don't'cha worry, it's nice and warm and dry There. There's a little bed in der for dem guests we sometime get. And your little friend will be safe and cozy right here in Thelma's old bed."

We were being separated.

"But I need to stay with Sunny!" Spirit insisted.

"There's only one bed in the shed, little girl," Thelma was getting a little annoyed with our pickiness.

We were being separated. I won't be able to organize our escape. I won't be able to protect her. To watch over her. I started sweating with cold fear. Fearful, terrible thoughts were pounding in my head.

"Ain't noth'n gonna happen to ya's," Thelma said to Spirit. "Not under Thelma's watch. OK?"

Spirit nodded.

Then Thelma opened the drawer in the small dresser. "Oh, here. There's Thelma's old teddy bear." She smiled and handed it to Spirit. It was a sorry looking teddy. It had a ripped arm and was missing an eye. Spirit took it from Thelma and thanked her shyly.

I gave Spirit a deep look. And gave her a hug and whispered in her ear, "We'll be fine. If anything happens, scream really hard. As hard as you can, OK?" She nodded.

Thelma started shuffling towards the door and lightly pushed me out. I turned my head backwards one more time to see Spirit standing in that saccharine pink room by the pink bed, holding the teddy bear in her hands and looking at me with distress. Thelma closed the door and smiled.

"Now then, let's take ya's to the shed now."

Before descending back to the bottom floor, she stopped at a small closet by the staircase and took out a few sheets. "The duvet is already there but ya'll need dem sheets."

We went down the stairs. I threw another look backwards, but the door to Spirit's room was closed.

From the living room I could hear Emanuel Jessop's snores. We turned left and went outside through the front door. The night was dark and clear. The air was clean and fresh. I suddenly felt deep sorrow for not being out there in the wilderness, hiding under the cover of darkness. Thelma was showing us nothing but kindness but that old man Jessop... he scared me.

We turned left and walked towards that smaller house which Thelma called the shed. The name in itself was a good enough reason to give me nightmares. Thelma opened the door and turned on the light. A single light bulb hung from the ceiling on a black cable. The shed was almost completely empty. The floor was swept but a little sandy. There was a small bed with a bare mattress that seemed to be a little dusty, a white duvet was folded on it and on top of the duvet there was a white pillow. A small dresser with a single drawer was by the bed. Two windows with plain, plaid, short curtains were set into two of the walls, one above the bed and the other across to the right. The room was, as Thelma said, warm and dry, with an old wooden scent that was also slightly dusty.

"Der ya're," Thelma said. She pushed the mattress with her hand. "Not squeaky!" She smiled. In her hands she still had the folded sheets and the pillow case. "Mind doin' it ya'rself?" she asked.

I shook my head. It was the least I could do to ease her burden.

She walked closer towards me with the linen in her hands. I put my hands up to receive them, but instead of just releasing and putting them in my arms, she kept holding them. She stood there almost on top of me, my hands under her hands still holding the linen. It was weird. "Ya know…" she said somewhat hesitantly, "Uncle Jessop… he ain't as bad as you might think."

Not that Uncle Jessop again.

"His wife Norma, my old aunty, mercy on her soul, she died a few years ago… and since den he… eh…. He's a little *lonely*."

It was the way she said lonely that got my attention. She tilted her head somewhat, as if she was sharing a secret with me. A secret which I supposedly understood.

"Ya know… everyone knows about what's going on in dat Natures farm, all dem parties and the… ya know… fooling' around…." She was so close to me, I could feel her bosom pressed against my hands. This talk about the farm confused me. What parties was she talking about? We only had birthday parties with our friends once a year. Everyone at the same time because we were all born in spring, every last one of us. And what did 'fooling around' mean? Another speech I could not decipher, but just like her uncle's monologue at the dinner table, it did not sound nice at all.

"So, ya know… he just needs, he just needs you to be… *nice* to him," she said.

I didn't think I was even given the opportunity not to be nice to him.

"So eh… d'ya understand?" she asked with a little smile and a weird twinkle in her eyes.

I didn't. But I suppose the small confused twitch I made with my eyebrows was enough for her to convince herself that I did.

"Wonderful." Finally, she let go of the linen. "Light switch is over der and… eh… so… good night!" She left me standing there confused and worried with a pile of linen and a deeply wary heart.

23 LIGHTS OUT

For a while I just stood still, the linen in my hands, looking at the closed door. I did not have any plan for escape yet. I knew I needed to sneak back into the night and get Spirit. I had no clue how deep Thelma's sleep was, or Uncle Jessop's. I was never that good in maintaining stealth mode, but I had a strong sense of dread; I just knew it in my heart that our lives depended on escaping this place.

There was no chair in the room so I sat on the naked bed. After a while I decided it would be nicer to sit on a made bed. I used the linen Thelma gave me. Everything was clean and smelled nice.

What now?

I had a suspicion that the shed might be watched from the house. Not turning the light off may seem odd to Thelma, so I switched it off.

I left the curtains wide open and laid myself on the bed. It was nice and comfortable. The sheets were soft to the touch. I thought if I just lay there, uncovered and looking at the stars outside through the window, I would keep myself awake and just pass the time until the main house fell asleep.

I was tired.

When was the last time I slept? It must have been two days ago. That night at the cornfield, but that wasn't real sleep, it was brief and disturbed. When was the last time I was in a bed?.... Three nights ago, I thought, or was it more... a week maybe? So much had happened I'd lost track of time.

I was so tired.

I'm not sure when and how but somehow, I sank into deep sleep. It was a very troubled sleep. I was back at the fence, and my mom was with me on top of the fence. Rosichi was about to touch the fence, she was holding a baby in her arms. The baby was puffy and lifeless like my mom's boys in the Sick Room. I was screaming to her, "Rosichi! Nooo!" She wasn't moving. Behind her, out of thin air appeared a man in a white suit, but I recognized him, I could tell it was the good-looking man. He said, "Don't touch the fence girl! Use the rug!" My mom started behaving stupidly, waving and giggling and letting her hair loose and fall on her shoulders, because she was so excited to see him... and she jumped off the fence! We were escaping but she jumped off to the wrong side – she jumped back into the farm... and I started shouting, "Momma! Momma! What are you doing? Don't go!" but she just took the hand of the good-looking man who was wearing the white suit and together they were walking back ... to the farm! I was in such fear I could almost taste it. Mom turned her head towards me and smiled a wicked little smile... "Look after Antim, Sunny... remember her..." she said slowly, like she was talking from inside a cloud. She turned her head back and kept walking hand in hand with the good-looking man, her thighs swaying from side to side. I was trying to scream to her but just then the White Suit woman appeared from behind a tree. I was trying to warn Rosichi... I screamed and screamed but no voice came out. She couldn't hear me. The woman grabbed Rosichi's head and smashed it into the fence.... I felt the electrical bolt go through my heart and suddenly found it hard to breathe... I was choking.... choking... choking....

I woke up in terror. I *was* choking, there was a hand on my mouth, covering my mouth and nose. My chest was being crushed by a heavy weight on top of me.

Like the bolt of electricity in my dream, I was fully into my senses now, I was wide awake, and I knew. I could feel his sour breath on me, one bony hand on my mouth choking me, the other feeling and grabbing at my private parts, like he was trying to find a key to a door.

"I'ma gonna put one in ya girl! Sweet Mercy," he kept saying over and over. "I'ma gonna put one in ya!" His mouth was at my breast. "Those fuckers at Natures don't have nothing on Emanuel Jessop! I'ma gonna suck that nectar right off ya... oh... yes. I'ma gonna put

one in ya, girl… Emanuel Jessop is gonna make ya happy right der...
Sweet Mercy!"

A feeling of pure, distilled hate was bubbling in me. It wasn't
completely new to me but I'm sure I have never felt it so strongly
before. Hate so pure and blazing. It was so strong that I felt it
streaming through my veins like it was a physical experience. It was
going through me, putting strength into every ounce of me. I felt like
I could kill him with my own hands just then.

I started fighting, I kicked and punched and tried to bite his hand on
my mouth. I put everything I had into resisting him, trying to get him
off me. For a skinny old git, he was rather heavy and resourceful. He
wasn't letting go of his prize that easily. I screamed. "Get off me! Get
off me!" and punched him in the face, aiming at his nasty-looking
eyes.

In return he withdrew the hand that was searching my private parts
and punched my face very hard with it. The slap of the Patrol
Woman at The Shed was a soft tickle in comparison to the force of
this one. A light flashed in my eye. A blinding pain paralyzed me for a
second, then I could sense it spreading from my cheekbone to my
mouth through my head and moving to my neck and shoulder. "You
little whore!" he was shouting at me, "You fucking little whore!" His
hand that was on my mouth was now at my throat and he was really
trying to choke me. I kept kicking and screaming but the world
started fading around me. I was still pushing and kicking but life was
slipping away.

In the fading dimness of the room I could just barely see a figure coming into the room. It was holding something. Then I could hear a very loud SMACK. Emanuel Jessop's body gave a little bounce of surprise. His grip at my throat loosened. He groaned and mumbled something. Another very loud SMACK had followed the first one, and then another. There was a sound of something cracking, and suddenly Emanuel Jessop's hand was completely off my throat and his body lay limp on top of me.

I took a deep breath. I was alive. At the side of the bed stood Spirit, a sizeable frying pan in her hand.

I rolled hateful Jessop off me and he fell to the floor. Blood was coming out of his ear. He looked dead.

"Thank you."

"Is he dead?" she asked, her voice shaking.

"Maybe…. That took a lot of strength," I said

She shrugged, her eyes wide open with terror, "I'm strong."

Gosh I loved her.

"We must get out of here!" I said in haste and jumped out of the bed, skipped over Jessop's pitiful naked body on the floor and took Spirit's shaking hand. She threw the frying pan on the bed.

The door to the shed crashed open and the light switch was flicked on. The sudden light, low as it was, was blinding. Thelma was standing in the door, her hair standing up in places, other bits held by gigantic rollers. She was wearing a white night tunic and a robe which was too small for her, so was left open at the front. It was peachy. She was panting.

For a moment I was thinking she'd be happy. She'd thank us. Her tyrant of an uncle was gone out of her miserable, subservient life.

"What the fuck just happened here?" she said, looking at her naked uncle on the floor. More and more blood was pooling under his head. The frying pan was lying, guilty, on the bed, blood and bits of hair stuck to it. "Is this Uncle Jessop?" she asked, a shocked look on her face. "What did ya's DO?" she stared at us, her eyes torn open. She pushed us aside and went to her uncle. She leaned towards him and touched him rather roughly. She then rolled him on his back. It was not a pretty sight. His eyes were open, staring at the ceiling. Blood poured from his ear and pooled on the floor. His nakedness was skeletal and grotesque. I gagged. She rose to her feet "Why?" he looked at me, her eyes filled with accusation. "Who da fuck d'ya think ya'are?" She was still panting. Her eyes wild. "Two fucking whores ya's escaped dem whore farm! You come to our house and this is how ya's repay our hospitality?"

Then she suddenly left the door and started walking to the house. Her steps were heavy and determined. With all her heaviness she was putting a lot of effort into it. You could tell she was making haste. Something was up with her.

We bolted through the door and started to run. Barefoot, clad only in our peachy robes we ran as fast as we could. Spirit had to grab the bottom of her robe in her hand so as not to trip over it. We ran into the dusty road through which the White Suits came to enquire about me that same afternoon. We were making a good distance very fast, but the house was still near enough for us to hear everything that was going on behind us.

I could hear the front door of the house crashing open. I could hear Thelma heaving herself out, facing the road. She was shouting at us, "Ya fucking whores! Come back here ya ungrateful fucking whores!" She was clicking something in her hands. There was a very loud bang and something was flying near us. It vibrated through the air.

"She's shooting at us!" Spirit screamed.

"Keep running, don't stop!"

In my mind I could hear Thelma's bragging words to the White Suit woman earlier that day. How she pointed her fingers at the White Suit and told her what a good a shooter she was, how she could blow eyes out of eye sockets, in the dark, and with her eyes closed. I was petrified. I did *not* want my eyes to be blown out of their sockets.

Thelma's shotgun clicked again in her big hands. Another shot was fired. Spirit and I kept running. The bullet missed us again.

In the distance, I could hear Thelma reloading. Another click. Another loud bang. I thought we'd outrun her rage when I felt a very sharp burn at the side of my right thigh, just under the buttock. It was like a fire rod cut into my flesh, very deeply. The pain was instantaneous and extreme.

"I'm hit!" I blurted in a mixture of surprise and anguish.

Somehow, I managed to keep running for a while longer, until the horror house was well behind us and only darkness resumed its presence all around.

We stopped running. I put my hand on the side of my thigh. I could feel the blood trickling down my leg; the pain was immense.

"I think it only scratched me," I said. But the pain was crippling.

"What do we do?" Spirit asked, deeply concerned.

I put my left hand on her shoulder and gave it a small reassuring squeeze. "We keep running."

24 THE CHASE

It wasn't running, really. I couldn't keep up. We were, at times, walking fast and other times slowly. Frequently I was practically dragging myself onwards. It wasn't just the deep, fresh, bleeding gunshot wound. That was the worst, but that pain seemed to have triggered and dragged back into the fore all the others. My face was throbbing, I thought my jaw may have been broken, my ankle was still very sore from the bad fall I took from the wall. Even my neck was still sore and burning from being violently choked. Every bone, muscle and cell in my body was hurting. To make everything even worse, we were barefoot.

At some point we decided to leave the dusty road that lead to and from the house and seemed to go on and on into the darkness, and took a turn right. We were walking on a plateau of old wild grass littered with old dried thorns. I could feel every single thorn that pricked my soles. The robe was doing a good job soaking up the blood but the bleeding did not stop and the further we went the less I was able to continue. I realized it was just a question of time before Spirit had to go on without me. Some protector I turned out to be… the other way around was more like it. *She* kept saving *me*.

Far on the horizon, an impressive vision was revealed. A city of twinkling lights. Buildings and high towers, lit up so magnificently. A real city. That was just a little bit exciting. I thought if I maintained a good pace, we might be able to reach this spectacular, shiny city by morning.

I could hear the rumble of an engine behind us. At first it was nothing more than a faint buzz, like a pestering insect, then louder and louder it grew, as the heavy vehicle drew nearer. The dusty road was far to our left but we had not distanced ourselves from it quite as much as I would have deemed safe. With everything I had in me I ran deeper into the wilderness. I could hear the vehicle was going very slowly. It was still quite dark. Far behind us I could just make out the two headlights of some sort of a Ute.

A despicable voice was shouting into the darkness, "I can see ya's foot prints in the sand and ya's blood trail ya little whore! I can smell it! Thelma's coming for ya, bitch!"

She'd picked up on our foot prints. I didn't think it could have been the blood. I couldn't have left a decent blood trail. I wasn't *that* injured… *Was I?* In any case, she'd be onto us in no time, I thought, with her shotgun and the crazed vengeance in her eyes.

We kept running straight into the nothingness. It was dark and we could hardly see anything ahead of us. I could hear the Ute maneuvering off the road and onto the plateau. The lights were now nearly on us.

"There ya're!" Thelma was yelping. She must have been really enjoying the hunt.

She was speeding now, the thrill of the chase at its peak. She must have been getting quite excited by the thought of mounting our heads on her wall pretty soon.

With one hand she held the wheel and with the other she was holding her shotgun. We ran in zigzags trying to avoid her. I was getting dizzier and dizzier. She fired a shot. The sound made me jump pretty badly. She was closer to us now than she was the first time when she got me. I knew that this was a challenge I had to somehow win - or we die. But how? How? I'd lost too much blood and couldn't even think clearly.

I was also running out of steam. You can depend on the force of sheer adrenaline to carry you for a while, but not forever. Even your primal survival instinct cannot do much for you when you vision is getting blurry.

She was gaining on us. Her Ute sounded old and rusty but it growled like a terrifying beast.

Another shot was fired. I thought I felt the vibrations in the air. Was I imagining it? She might have missed me by only a few inches.

That was the end.

I couldn't run any more. I might just drop to the ground where I was. I might just let her kill me and get it over and done with.

I remember falling. I wasn't shot, I just fell. My body just ran out of fuel. I hit the ground hard, bashing my head, adding more pain to that which I already had. Everything unfolded in slow motion. I could hear Spirit shouting my name. I sensed her running to me. I saw her feet at my face. She was shouting my name. My eyes were open but I couldn't really see very much, I couldn't even open my mouth. I could hear the engine roaring so close it was almost on me. I could hear Thelma's yelping and yowling. I realized she was trying to run me over. I could feel Spirit grabbing my arm and towing me hard out of the way. I could hear the Ute. It felt like it was missing me by only an inch, it was so close I could feel the warmth of the wheels on the side of my body and the splattering of soil on me as it went past. Then there was a scream. Then an enormous CRASH. And then another CRASH. Then there was a colossal BANG and a ball of fire rose to the sky. A wave of heat engulfed us and I could hear Spirit shrieking. Then there was a minor bang. Some cracklings. And then silence.

Spirit was at my side crying.

"I'm not dead yet," I managed to say.

Then the world went dark.

25 THE SPARKLY CITY

I opened my eyes again as dawn broke and delicate light was illuminating the sky again. That moment when the world wakes up to a new day, still a little dark, still wiping its sleeping webs, was always a moment of sheer beauty and of hope, but I had very little of that for myself that morning.

"Hey." Spirit was at my side.

"Hey," I answered. Still numb, heavy and dizzy. "What happened?"

Spirit thought about it for a moment. "Sweet Mercy," she finally said, smiling.

She held my arm and helped me up to my feet. The world was dancing around me. A few meters from where I fell to the ground was an unseen pit. It was quite wide and deep, probably a crater caused a long time ago by one of those catastrophic earthquakes we learned about in the community room. In the darkness it was completely invisible. We might have fallen straight into it had we kept running. Instead we were still alive, which couldn't be said about Thelma. The Ute was smashed to smithereens at the bottom of the crater, blackened and smoking. Relieved as I was to see this, it wasn't a pleasant sight. The smell of burnt petrol and smoking flesh was pungent.

"Are you OK?" I asked Spirit.

"I got a little burn on my back," she said. "But I'm OK."

She was a good liar. I almost believed her.

"Look there, Sunny," Spirit pointed beyond the smoking crater, "Doesn't it look wonderful?"

Now that the many layers of darkness had evaporated, ahead of us loomed the city. No more twinkling with night lights, but grey and domineering. Clad with glassed windows everywhere, sparkling in the early daylight. High risers and sky scrapers, just like in the pictures we had in the community room. I used to be mesmerized by those pictures. They seemed so out of this world to a farm girl like me.

"We need to find a Sick Room," I said, "in there. It will be dangerous but we must, because I just don't know how long I can carry on."

We had to get around the crater which appeared to be a substantial obstruction in our way. We moved very slowly. I was practically dragging myself.

"I'm really sorry, Spirit."

"About what?

"I'm sorry I didn't take better care of you until now... Of us."

"You took great care of me, Sunny!" she seemed surprised.

"I seem to be an utter failure at leading us to safety."

"That's not your fault, Sunny." She was still holding the lower end of her peachy robe in her hands. Her face was all muddy again, her hair covered with soil and dust. I could see her feet were as badly bruised as mine. She wasn't even complaining. She seemed to be fully concentrating on the city ahead.

"Do you think there even *is* a safe place for us?" she suddenly wondered. "What if there is something about us... because we are different... what if everywhere we go they would try to kill us?"

That thought filled me with fright and sadness. "We are not different," I said.

"We have those things in our hands..."

"That's because Natures think they own us. They put it there without even asking us. But they can't own us... we are... ourselves! We... belong to *us*!" I tried to explain. The thought of living in a world where not even a single person cared whether we lived or died was too depressing to bear.

I was getting tired of walking, tired of talking and tired of thinking. I looked at the city and I knew, I just knew, that I could not make it that far.

"Spirit, you need to promise me something!"

She looked at me with her big, slightly slanted eyes.

"You need to promise me that you will keep going without me!"

"Sunny! But..." she tried to protest.

"No, listen to me. Please. You must keep going. I know there is safety out there. I know it. Remember me?... *I smell danger from miles away*... Well that's not even true, really.... But this one I just *know*. You must go on and find it. You are strong and smart and capable. You can do it."

"I'm not going to leave you, Sunny! Please stop..."

I wasn't listening. "You are also a very cute girl and people really like that... You can use that... it can help you."

She didn't like that last bit. "Thelma was trying to kill me, even though I was *cute*."

"I think she was trying to kill me mostly... you were just collateral damage... If I died I think she would have kept you."

"Well then I would rather be dead!" she blurted.

"Even when you're angry you're cute," I chuckled, but it only hurt

179

my lungs and my throat so I stopped.

The more we walked around the crater the more it felt that we were moving further away from the city. At places the gap between the two sides of the pit narrowed but never enough to be able to attempt crossing it with a harrowing jump. Not that I would have tried that. I did not have the strength. In fact, I was fading fast. I could hear cars not too far away in the distance. I could even feel them; their engines roared and caused the ground to tremble lightly. There must have been so many cars on that road, I found it hard to imagine.

I didn't make it to the elusive road. Instead, for a while I felt like I was floating. Drifting. I couldn't see the ground, or the city, or Spirit, or my filthy feet, dripped with blood and repeatedly cut with thorns. They were all awash with bright white light, shapeless and soulless. I couldn't hear a thing. Not the cars in the distance, not my feet meeting the ground, not Spirit's breathing, not my own breaths. Everything was overshadowed by a strong ringing in my ears, inside my head. I couldn't even hear my own body hit the ground. I couldn't even hear Spirit's screaming. I could only imagine it, somewhere behind the whiteness and the bells.

Then, everything went black.

26 BEYOND THE DARKNESS

Beyond the darkness, I had another dream. A very weird one.

In my dream I could see Spirit. She was running, still with that ridiculous peachy robe on her that she had to hold in her hands not to trip over. She was sliding down some benign looking ridge, sliding and rolling. She was screaming and waving her arms. A shiny black road stretched alongside her. Behind her, it went far into the hazy horizon, and in front of her it curved forward all the way to the outskirts of the tall grey city. There were many cars driving to and from the city in both directions. So many. And so colorful. I had only ever seen white cars before. They were going pretty fast too. I could feel the fear in my dream, like it was a physical being, standing right there with us. I also wasn't too sure who *I* was in that dream. Maybe Fear *was* me.

The cars wouldn't stop. I could see Spirit crying and waving and begging. It was as if no one could see her. I sensed her desperation.

Out of nowhere, there was my mom. She looked so beautiful, determined, standing tall, her hair loose on her shoulders blowing lightly in the breeze, everything about her was so impressive. There was almost a golden tint to her… like she brought the sun. What was she doing there?

"Mom?…. Mom!" She couldn't hear me.

Mom looked at Spirit. I don't know if Spirit could see her, but she stopped waving around. Then, Stella just went straight into the road. I'm pretty sure that I *was* Fear, because I could feel myself imploding. What was she doing?

She just stood there, in the middle of the road, and she raised her arm, her hand stretched, signaling the cars to stop.

And, bizarre as it seemed, a car did stop. A little blue one. It slowed down and then it pulled over on the side of the road next to Spirit. The door opened and a nicely dressed old looking woman looked at Spirit with some interest and concern.

"Can I help you dear?" she asked in a kind voice.

"I need to find a Sick Room," Spirit said.

"Do you mean a hospital, dear?"

Spirit nodded. We didn't use this word at the farm, but we knew it existed. "My friend is dying."

"Oh, dear," the old looking woman replied. "Jump in, I'll take you to the hospital."

I could see Spirit hesitate, but my mom was already in the car, sitting in the back seat, signaling to Spirit with her finger to get in.

I don't know how but, in my dream, I could follow the car from above. I suppose dreams are always weird like that.

I followed the blue car that kept going straight into the city. From up above where Fear was, the contour of the city reminded me of photos of beautiful brides in an old brides' magazine we had in the community room. Like the hem of a long veil, the city announced itself with some small-looking houses, few and far between. Then some blocks of what looked like large grouping of shops and parking spaces, followed with rows and rows of two-storey houses. Then, just as the veil rose up to reveal a beautiful sparkly dress, so the city rose too. Buildings of unimaginable height, covered in shiny, sparkly, tinted windows. They were so impressive, so commanding. The blue car became almost a dot on the ground far below. The main road now branched off into an artwork of smaller roads, like veins through a body. Each road had decorative white markings on it. When Fear dived back to the car I could see people. The streets were filled with them. They were walking alongside the roads where the cars were, and using the white markings to cross from one side to the other. When they stepped onto the markings cars would stop. It was fascinating. Like observing a well-coordinated dance between people and cars.

The blue car stopped in front of a large, grey-looking, wide building with a plain façade. Mom wasn't inside it any more.

"This is the hospital, dear," the woman said.

Spirit looked at her. She was a bit lost. I suppose she did not think a Sick Room would be this big.

The woman did not offer to help any further, she just nodded to Spirit to get out.

In my dream, I saw Spirit for what she was, a lost young child walking through corridors of sick rooms, full of people. She was wearing nothing but a worn out, dirty, peachy robe, her feet covered with bleeding cuts, her face filthy, her hair a mess, big tears in her eyes. No one saw her. No one looked at her. She was transparent. Fear shrieked when men and women in white suits walked past her. But something about their white suits was a little different from the ones at the farm. Different length, different style. These men and women all had stethoscopes around their necks.

"I need help! Please, I need help!" Spirit was rushing through the corridors, trying to draw attention to herself. Everyone seemed to be so busy. No one was listening. "Please! My friend is dying!" she tugged on people's sleeves, but they shook their hands off. One of the busy men paused for a brief moment and told her to go to reception.

Where was reception?

Spirit was lost. She started crying.

Behind her came Stella. Tall and proud and golden, with the sun in her, just like before. She walked past Spirit. She approached a woman in blue uniform that was sifting through paperwork. The woman looked just as busy as anyone else. She had shoulder-length blonde hair that sort of curved up at the end. She wore a black hair-band just above her very short fringe. She had a red lipstick on. Stella stood in front of the woman. She touched her with her gold-tinted hand, and there was a glow of light, like the sun was shining through her and into the woman. The woman stopped sifting through the documents. She looked at her hand with some bewilderment. Stella was still touching her, but she was looking now directly at Spirit. The woman raised her head. She saw Spirit. She dropped the papers and rushed to her. Spirit was still crying. The woman smiled at her. She had a name tag attached to the dash of her top, it read, "Rose." Rose touched Spirit's hand.

"Can I help you?"

"My friend is dying," Spirit was sobbing.

The woman, Rose, seemed worried. "Where is your friend?"

"Outside the city… there is a crater above the road… far…"

"If you came with me in the ambulance, would you be able to show me where to go?"

Spirit nodded.

"Come with me," Rose said. She used a hand-held talking machine to ask for an ambulance to be ready for her immediately, one of the four-wheel-drive ones, because the patient was on the plains.

In my dream, Spirit and Rose disappeared inside a green-yellow van with big black wheels that started yowling as soon as the car was on the move. Lights were flashing on its roof.

Stella looked at them from the entrance of the hospital. And then she looked directly at me. She saw me.

"Sunny!" she said.

And the world was black again.

27 AWAKE

I'm not sure what woke me. Maybe it was those perpetual mechanical beeps in my ear.

I cracked my eyes open. In the beginning all I could see was bright light and some unidentifiable shadows. Slowly, things became sharper and the shadows wore recognizable shapes.

I found myself in a white room. I was lying in a white bed, covered with white bedsheets and a blanket. There was a wide window to my left. Through it, I could see blue skies and some green treetops swaying lightly in the wind. The trees cast an ever-changing shadow into the room. I could feel myself. I was not floating. I was not dreaming. I could see my left ankle was firmly held in some sort of a cast. There were bandages around both my feet. I could feel my face. It was sore. There was a bandage on my right cheek that went all the way down to my chin and onto my neck. I could feel stiffness in my bones and heaviness in my lungs. I could feel the side of my right thigh. It was very painful. My entire body was throbbing. But at the same time, I was somehow serene. I was hooked to a machine that beeped every few seconds. A plastic tube was inserted into a vein in my right arm. I followed it with my eyes all the way up where it ended with a flimsy looking red bag. I guessed they were pumping blood into me. To the right of me there was another white bed. I tried to turn my head but my face was so incredibly sore that I could barely stretch my neck. I grimaced with pain. I couldn't see who was in the other bed.

"Sunny?"

It was Spirit.

"Heyyyyy," I said. My mouth was heavy, my tongue sticky, my voice hoarse and raspy. Gosh I was in so much pain.

Into the room came a woman. She was wearing blue. Her hair was blonde, shoulder length, curving up at the edges. She had a black hair band on top of her very short fringe and a hot red lipstick.

"Rose?" I asked.

The woman's face lit.

"Hello... Yes, I am Rose, your head nurse. I didn't know you'd woken up before...." she said with a smile.

I hadn't.

"Are you in pain sweetheart?" she asked me.

I nodded.

She grabbed a syringe then unscrewed some of the tubes that were attached to me through the vein and inserted the content of the syringe inside the tube. I could feel the coldness of the content flowing through my vein.

After that everything went dark again.

28 AWAKE. AGAIN

The next time I woke up I was still in the same white room, lying in the same white bed, covered with white bedsheets and a blanket. I realized then, with some relief, that I did not dream the previous time.

The curtains on the wide window to my left were drawn together. They had pretty red flowers embroidered on them. Through a very narrow gap between them I could see that the sky was dark. It must have been night time. My left ankle was still firmly held by a cast but the bandages around my feet were gone. I wriggled my toes. It did not hurt. My face was still sore. The bandage was still there but I could sense that it was not stretched further than my chin this time. The side of my right thigh, where I was shot by a deranged Thelma, was still immensely painful. I moved my hand, to realize that I was indeed still hooked to the beeping machine and to the plastic tube in my vein. This time, as I followed the line with my eyes, I saw that the liquid inside the flimsy bag was sort of colorless. To the right of me there was still another bed. I could turn my neck and see it. Spirit was still there. She was sleeping. I felt such relief, I thought I had just wet myself, but it was the unfamiliar feeling of the catheter that was attached to me.

Rose walked into the room with some paperwork. She was checking all sort of charts at the side of my bed when she noticed I was awake.

"Hi Sunny," she smiled.

"Hi Nurse Rose," I said. My throat was so sticky, it took a lot of effort to say just those three words. I wasn't thirsty, I just felt dry. My voice was still hoarse and raspy.

"How are you feeling? Still in much pain?"

"Yes."

"You are doing very well," she said. "I shall ease your pain again."

"Wait… can I please have some water?"

She took a small plastic cup already at my bedside and walked to the other side of the room, beyond Spirit's bed. There was a small sink there. She filled it with water and got back to me. She put a small straw in the cup. "Here you go Sunny. Drink slowly."

The water was cool and refreshing. My throat felt immediately better.

"How is Spirit?" I asked.

"She's doing very well," Rose smiled, "a very brave little girl." She said it softly. Fondly.

"Why is she here?"

"She had cuts to her feet and some burns to her back. Not severe. She will be fully recovered in no time," she was still smiling. Her smile seemed genuine. "Don't worry."

I *was* worried. I could feel worry eating at me. But I couldn't remember why I was supposed to be so worried. I tried to remember… there was some danger. But what was it?... My brain was so foggy. My body still so sore…

"Here, I'll put more of the sleeping gift into your system," Rose said, and started injecting me with whatever it was in that syringe.

I could feel the coolness of it going through. A man opened the door and peeked in. "Oh, excuse me Rose, would you please come out for a second when you're done?"

What was he wearing…?

"Sure, Doctor Appledorn," she said and giggled, "just give me a sec."

White Suits! I remembered!

"Wait!"

Too late. Everything went dark.

29 THE NURSE AND THE DOCTOR

The next time I woke up, I was still in the same room. I was still lying in the same white bed, covered with white bedsheets and a blanket. The curtains were open and in streamed the light of a clear sunny day. My left ankle was free. A small stretchy bandage that looked more like a tight sock was covering it now. I turned it here and there, it was stiff but not painful. My face was not sore either. There was no bandage on it. The side of my right thigh was still sore but not as bad as it was. I could actually move and sit up in bed. I was still hooked to the IV line but not to the machine. The beeping had gone. And so was Spirit's bed. Instead there was a couch to the side of me. Spirit was sitting there, dwarfed by its substantial size, almost swollen by it. She noticed me and jumped up with joy.

"Sunny!" she exclaimed with such overwhelming joy, and leaned down for a hug.

She wasn't heavy but my stiff body still felt a bit sore, so I let out quite an involuntary "UMPH". She got off me immediately.

193

"Sorry!"

"No, don't worry! I'm feeling so much better."

Her smile was the biggest I had ever seen.

"I was so worried," she said, "I thought I lost you…." Tears came up to her eyes. "I thought you'd died."

I smiled. "I'm here… and again it is thanks to you that I made it!" I took her hand and gave it a squeeze. "You must be my guardian angel."

She giggled.

"But, how are you? You had burns?"

"Oh, no… not too bad. It was the explosion of Thelma's car. It burned my back a little… I'm fine."

"Are you sure?"

"Yup. My scars are tiny and I only put on some oil before bedtime now," she said.

"Spirit… how long have we been here?"

She thought about it for a while. "Uh… about three and a half weeks, I think."

What? I jumped up in my bed, the side of my body immediately reminding me why I was still *in* bed. I groaned in pain.

"Be careful, Sunny!" Spirit said with more than a bit of scolding. "You are still not recovered. I'm not sure you had your stitches removed yet…. That was quite the wound you had there!"

"Almost a month?"

"Well… yes… you should have seen the state of you!"

"Spirit… the White Suits… they must know we are here!"

"Don't worry…. We are guarded."

"Guarded? By whom?"

"Rose."

"Rose? The nurse?"

"Yes. And her husband Doctor Jonathan."

"Who?"

"Don't worry, Sunny… everything is all right."

"Stop saying that for a second!" I said impatiently. "What do you mean they are guarding us?"

"They know…." Spirit said quietly, "about us… being from Natures."

"You *told* them?" Gosh this was only getting worse.

"Well, it wasn't exactly hard for them to find out with those stupid things still stuck in our arms!" she said defensively.

I sighed. I took a deep breath in. So, they knew. That made us a sitting prey. Why even bother healing me when I was going to be taken back to the farm only to be broken again?

I looked at Spirit. She was offended by my anger. "I'm sorry," I said. "I was just… surprised by the whole thing." I took a moment to think. "So, how exactly are they guarding us?"

Spirit looked at me with her slightly slanted eyes, like she was measuring my sincerity. I guess I passed the test because she told me.

Apparently, in the city, the authority of Natures Farmers is only limited. Unlike the farm where they are rulers supreme, here they couldn't just barge into the hospital and demand us back. Even if we were their 'property', there were all sorts of medical conventions that forbade it. It also turned out that Nurse Rose and her husband Doctor Jonathan were no great fans of Natures and their irresponsible breeding program; even though it was an organic farm, it was still 'not OK'.

I looked at Spirit as she was reciting all this to me. Half of it sounded like gobbledygook. Not quite as bad as Uncle Jessop's, but close enough.

"So, let me make sure I understand…" I tried to make sense of it all. "Nurse Rose and her husband Jonathan know who we are and why we are here, but the White Suits *also* know we are here…."

"Yes."

"But Rose and Jonathan are not allowing the White Suits to take us? They are just keeping us here?"

"Yes."

"Locked up?"

"What? No! We aren't locked up. The toilets are outside in the corridor!"

"So, they are keeping us… because I am still a patient?"

"Yes."

"What happens when I am all better, then?"

"I believe I can answer that." Rose came through the door.

30 THE PLAN

She closed the door behind her and came close to the bed.

Spirit smiled at her. Rose put her hand around Spirit's shoulder and patted her for a brief moment. I wasn't prepared for such... familiarity between them. I don't know why but it totally made me resent that nurse woman.

"How are you feeling, Sunny?"

"Super-duper... what about that explanation?"

"Sunny!"

"That's OK, Spirit." Rose smiled. Her voice was calm and mellow. "I can explain." She moved to the other side of the bed from where she could face both me and Spirit at the same time.

"We know that Natures farmers and scientists are after you. They arrived at the hospital about two days after you were hospitalized here. But we... Doctor Jonathan and I, were suspicious you were runaways even before they came here.... From your raggedy robes and your wounds... We assumed you had a very rough time escaping." She paused and looked at me. It was a kind look. I found it hard to maintain that level of suspiciousness with her. "It only took a simple test to verify that," she said, and pointed at my wrist. "You are marked. These farmers are relentless. They have invested a lot of money into you and would not let you slip away from them that easily." She put a gentle hand on my shoulder. "They don't see you as two young, innocent girls. To them you are business. Money."

"If they take us back they are going to hurt us," I said. "They hurt our friends... a lot... and they forced them to..." Tears filled my eyes and choked me.

"We know about the breeding program. It is completely irresponsible. No other farm starts breeding with girls so young!"

"Other farms? There are other farms like Natures?"

"Natures has lots of farms... you probably came from the one they own down south. It's a small boutique one, but all of Natures farms are organic, which means the quality of their milk is far superior to that of their competitors." She smiled kindly. "Also, more expensive."

"Nurse Rose," Spirit said, "we don't want to go back there!"

"And we won't let them take you. We are against that kind of terrible treatment. So young! Jonathan and I have discussed it the first day you arrived, that we won't send you back. Mind you, the same protocol that entrusts you to us and allows us to keep you here while you are medically treated, also forces us to hand you over as soon as you are well enough."

She leaned even closer. "And they will demand you! They already have. One of their leading scientists, an insufferable woman, came here at least ten times already asking to see your charts, Sunny. I had to falsify some of them just to make your condition seem worse than you actually were… That is illegal… but a risk worth taking." She was looking at Spirit while saying that.

I was not expecting anyone to do something so out of the ordinary just to save my neck. It was… confusing.

"What are you going to do?" I asked, truly bewildered.

"Well, we need to remove your data key from your wrists," she said, "as soon as possible."

"Why didn't you already?"

"Because this is not something that we can do here… Legally you are still Natures' property. We cannot just openly interfere with you in ways that are not directly related to your injuries." She gave us a wicked smile and lowered her tone even further, "But that doesn't mean we can't do it outside the hospital."

"Where?"

"At our house. We have a clinic. It's not a surgery room, but digging that little chip out of you would not require full anesthesia, only local numbing should do it. We're willing to risk it."

"Why?"

"Because…" Rose hesitated. She raised her eyes and looked at Spirit. "We feel it is the right thing to do."

I realized it then. They were not risking everything for me. It was for Spirit. There was something about her.

"When will you get us out of here?"

"We think it will take you another week to be able to walk freely without pain in your side."

"A week?"

"We don't want to rush it, or we might look suspicious," she said. "Remember that Natures is a big, wealthy corporation. They have money, they have power, they have politicians under their pay… messing with them is dangerous. As your main carers, we are being watched."

"So, what do we do now?"

"You get better."

I had a week.

Nurse Rose left the room and Spirit sat back down on the couch. I only then noticed her clothes. She had a very cute dress on. It was white with purple butterflies and a very lavish purple rim. The sleeves were short and puffy. Her hair was clean and done in two plaits, both tied with beautiful purple bows that matched her dress. She had white ballerina shoes on. She was so pretty.

"That's a nice dress," I said.

She smiled, and stroked it playfully. "It was a gift from Rose and Jonathan."

I bet it was too.

"It was nice of them."

"They are nice people, Sunny."

"Did Rose do your hair?"

"Yes."

"It's nice."

What an awkward conversation. I don't know what was bothering me so much. Rose seemed nice, and genuine. I really didn't want to, but truth was I had trust in her. I couldn't explain to myself what was off... but the more I tried to find a fault with Rose I only came up with a single conclusion. Now that Spirit had a replacement mother, she may not need a replacement older sister any more.

31 KIDNAPPED

A man in grey overall walked into the room. He had grey hair to match and a friendly smile.

"Good evening ladies," he said politely, "would you be having your dinner in the room?"

"Yes," Spirit said.

"No problem, Miss."

He turned away and came back with two trays. One he laid at my bedside and the other he handed to Spirit to hold.

"Thank you, Simon" Spirit said.

"You have a good evening now, Miss."

The man left.

"*Simon?*" I had to wonder.

"I know everyone. I've been here for ages," she said.

"Where do you sleep?"

"This couch opens to a bed. I don't like it when it's opened all the time. It makes me feel like I'm sick."

The dinner arrived and looked so beautiful. I hadn't eaten a proper meal since that horror night at Thelma and Uncle Jessop's. It smelled nice and warm. Pea soup with nice wholemeal bread, roasted cauliflower, chickpea fritters and to finish, a small personal tub of chocolate ice cream. I took the small ice cream tub in my hand and looked at it, suspiciously.

"Oh, you have to try it, Sunny!" Spirit urged me enthusiastically. "It is so delicious! It's made with something called..." she paused thinking, then blurted "Coconut cream!"

I only ate a small portion of everything and was very full in the end.

"Did you finish your ice cream?" Spirit asked.

"No."

She finished it for me, licking the tub to the very last drop, which left her with a grand chocolaty moustache and a big smile.

Being full made me sleepy again.

"Tell me how you got help," I asked Spirit.

She was very excited to tell me everything, and I was very keen to hear, but I think I heard her up to, "I waved and waved, but no one stopped! They just kept driving past me…" when I fell back to sleep. I sort of knew the rest anyway.

It was night time when I woke up again. Alarm was raging in the pit of my stomach. Someone was in the room, moving around a little clumsily but in great rush. It was dark in the room but enough light from the corridor fell into the room and my heart stopped. I could see his clothes and he was coming straight at me. A White Suit.

He stated disconnecting me from the IV line. Before I could even scream, he plucked the IV line out of my vein. Blood came out and he pushed a cotton ball on it, very hard, with one hand and covered my mouth with the other. I was screaming by then, but his hand was big and my screams were lost.

They are here. They are stealing us back to the farm, to The Shed. So much for Rose and her husband 'guarding us.'

I reached for Spirit. I tried to call her, to wake her. Get her attention.

I started kicking, like I did that night when vile Emanuel Jessop surprised me in my sleep. Only this time my right side was out of action and completely useless. Kicking with one leg was more comical than useful, and did not seem to do much at all. The man was strong. He was years younger than Jessop.

"Shhhhh!" he shooshed me, "stop fighting!"

I didn't stop. I kept screaming under his hand. I tried to call to Spirit.

To Rose. Someone! Help! Help me!

"Be quiet!" he ordered again, his voice a loud but very demanding whisper.

I was not going to go back to the farm! They will not take me alive! My heart was pounding so hard, I thought I might die right there from a heart attack. It would have been better than being kidnapped and taken back to the farm.

The White Suit leaned lower towards me, "I am Doctor Jonathan Appledorn, Rose's husband. We must remove you now. Stop screaming! Natures agents are coming up right now to take you."

What?

"If I remove my hand, promise not to scream. I will show you my Doctor's ID tag."

I nodded.

He removed his hand and pulled his Doctor's ID. In spite of the narrow stream of light into the room I could see that his ID was indeed for Doctor Jonathan Appledorn, and his photo matched his looks.

I was still breathing very hard. Doctor Jonathan was putting things in a small bag and ripping off the papers that were clipped to the end of my bed.

How come Spirit was still sleeping?

"Spirit?" I whispered.

"She is already in the car, waiting for you," he said with haste.

I could see that her bed was clear and folded back into a couch.

"OK," he said, "I have everything I need. Now all I need is to move you. I can't take you with the bed so you will have to walk."

I hadn't walked in almost a month.

"You will be a little dizzy getting up and your wound may hurt, but we can't wait a moment longer."

I nodded.

He came to the side of the bed and pulled me up, helping me to lay my feet on the floor. I was wearing nothing but a thin hospital gown. I don't know what it is about running away, but it seemed to always consist of a basic underlying fashion requirement - wear little.

Jonathan took my left arm and pulled me up underneath him. My right side was hurting, but I could walk.

"As fast as you can," he said. "And please don't make a sound."

We got to the door. "We'll take the service elevator," he whispered.

He peeked out first, then we turned quickly left, into the corridor. I walked as fast as I could, half leaning on him. We must have looked very funny. The corridor was brightly lit but rooms were mostly shut, and those that were open were dark. Behind us was a nurse station where some of Rose's colleagues were shuffling papers and having hushed chats. One of them may have been saying something funny as the other nurse was laughing heartily, making an obvious attempt to keep her voice down. They paid no attention to us.

We walked all the way to the end of the corridor where Jonathan used his ID to call the service elevator. He kept looking very nervously back to the other side of the corridor. The service elevator was slow to arrive. I had never waited for an elevator before, but due to Jonathan's restlessness I soon realized that this one was especially slow.

A small light flickered above the elevator door. The door made a very small 'Ping' sound. Still it took a long time for it to actually arrive and open up.

Meanwhile on the other side of the corridor, another 'Ping' was heard. I sensed Jonathan's body becoming rigid. "Fuck," he blurted.

Out of the visitors' lift came three White Suits. Two men and a woman. *That* woman.

They may have had just a brief chance to notice us going inside the service lift on the far side from them, but that was all it took.

I could hear them breaking into a run. "Hey! Stop right there! Stop. Right. There!"

Jonathan nearly threw me into the lift and pressed the button that said B1.

Nothing happened.

I could hear them getting closer. One of the nurses was heard shouting, "What is this? Who are you? Where do you think you are going? Come back here!" There was a small buzz sound, like something was being zapped. Then someone fell to the ground. The running continues.

"One One Five Seven Two! You stop right there!"

My body was covered with cold sweat. I felt dizzy. Jonathan kept pressing the B1 button, almost hysterically. "C'mon! C'mon!" he kept saying.

Slowly, leisurely the doors of the service lift started to close.

"Stop! Stop right there!" the woman White Suit kept shouting.

The service elevator's door was nearly fully shut when the White Suit woman reached us and managed to stick her hand into the slim gap that remained between the doors, keeping them from fully closing.

"One One Five Seven Two you are MINE!" she was shouting, clasping the door, trying to get the doors to open again. "MINE!"

The doors were beginning to yield.

The surge of distilled fiery hate that came over me only once before in such a powerful wave washed over me again. There was no way that I was going to allow those doors to open again.

I leaped onto the door and grabbed the woman's fingers and with all my rage and hate and desperation I twisted them backwards. I could hear her screaming with pain. In an instinct she removed her hand from the door. "You BITCH!" she was screaming at the narrowing gap.

Not very original. I've been called that before.

"My name is Sunny!" I said to the narrowing gap.

The doors closed.

We were moving.

32 AN ENCOUNTER IN THE PARKING LOT

The elevator hummed as it made its way down.

Jonathan was pacing around very nervously. "C'mon! C'mon!"… He took his glasses off and gave them a wipe. His eyes were very blue, but his hands were trembling a little.

I was leaning on the hand rail that went all around the large metallic space. Above the handrail, large aluminum plates decorated all sides. They were shiny enough for me to be able to see my hazy reflection. I was a complete mess. I realized I'd lost a lot of weight in the short time since we'd escaped the farm, and I was incredibly pale.

"Ping!" the elevator announced we reached our destination. The doors opened to reveal a wide concreted space full of parked cars. Right outside the elevator landing, a silver car was awaiting, its engines on. Jonathan grabbed my arm and semi-walked, semi-carried me at high speed to the car. He opened the door and helped me into the back seat. Spirit wasn't there. She wasn't in the car! The man had lied to me!

Jonathan practically threw himself into the passenger seat. "They almost got us," he shouted to Rose who was at the wheel. "I think I've been seen... I think they'll have an easy job recognizing me." Then, a little bewilderedly he looked at her and added anxiously, "Go! Go! Go!"

Rose did not move her feet. The car remained stationary.

"Where is Spirit?" I screamed. "Where is she?"

Rose's hands were shaking. She was whimpering uncontrollably.

"Where is Spirit?" Jonathan asked, looking quite stunned at the back seat. He sounded surprised and worried.

"They took her!" she cried.

"What?" he was nearly shouting

"Who took her? Where is she?" I screamed, absolutely hysterically, wild with worry and suspicion of these two who'd just kidnapped me and thrown me into their car.

"Natures people," Rose was crying. "They grabbed her from the car, we were already down here, waiting for you." Big tears were rolling down her cheeks.

I lost control of myself. I was so confused. Who were these people? Were they truly so upset or just darn good actors? What did they want with me? Were they about to hand me over to the White Suits? And where the heck was Spirit?

I did the only thing my body knew how to do in such distressing moments; I opened the door and bolted. I started running.

I could hear the car door opening and Jonathan shouting behind me, "Sunny! Get back here!"

I kept running deep into the concreted dungeon. Checking every car, I passed to see if Spirit was there. I wasn't even sure what I was looking for exactly. I didn't think she would just be sitting and waiting for me in a car somewhere, but I acted on complete instinct.

"Sunny! Sunny! Wait! Come back!" I could still hear Jonathan shouting behind me, his shouts echoing in the large hall. They could not follow me. I was running against traffic, facing cars that were approaching me head on. Rose and Jonathan were almost immediately blocked by an approaching car.

I got further and further away from them. The path was lit by artificial, cold light. Cars were parked everywhere, forming together a giant, faceless mass of dark metal all around me. Further ahead in front of me I could spot, to my horror, a white car parked in the middle of the path, completely blocking traffic from both directions. I kept running towards it, but I slowed down somewhat. I could feel in my gut that the car was menacing. As I got closer and closer, my heart was hammering so hard, I could feel my chest aching. There were two hands against the side window of the back seat, pounding it from inside.

Spirit!

She was screaming. Her hands kept hitting the window. I could hear her muffled voice.

I threw myself at the door. "SPIRIT!!!! SPIRIT!!!" I screamed, trying frantically to open it. The door was locked.

I could see Spirit's face inside, covered in tears. She kept pounding with her hands on the window.

"SPIRIT!" I cried. Big, desperate tears were chocking me. "Open the door!" I hit the window of the front seat. A man was blankly staring at me from inside. He wore a white suit. "OPEN THE DOOR!" I screamed. My voice was breaking. He turned his head away from me. I was losing my mind. Spirit stopped. Her hands were just stuck to the window. She was crying.

"Spirit!" I sobbed, fighting to catch my breath. I laid my hands on the window from the outside, hers matching mine from within. I didn't know what to do.

Then Spirit started pounding the window again. She was screaming.

I wiped my tears.

She was not just pounding, she was pointing. Pointing and screaming, and hitting the window with complete desperation. Her muffled screams sounded a lot like "Sunny! Sunny!"

She was pointing.

Something behind me.

I looked at the window. In the vague reflection, I could clearly see someone was approaching me from behind. Was it Jonathan? All in on the conspiracy to hurt us?

I turned my head, my hands still on the window. It wasn't him, it was her. She was running towards me, the White Suit woman from the farm. In her hand she held a syringe with a large needle. The same as the one that was used to take Dawn down.

I didn't even scream, I was so empty by then. The White Suit woman pounced at me, the syringe in her hand. She was trying to hit my neck with the needle. Somehow, squirming and twisting myself, I managed to get out of the way.

Spirit was screaming in the car. Her hands still pounding the window in desperation. But between me and the White Woman there was only silence. All I could see was the needle and the ferocity in her eyes. I defended myself with my arms as best I could, blocking her every attempt to sting me.

Then, in a brief moment, she outsmarted me. With a quick move she managed to grab my hair and pulled it very hard, making me bend backwards towards her with immense pain. She was strong. I winced with pain and despair. The needle was almost at my neck.

But then, without a warning, a WHACK! And her hold on my hair was released. The syringe fell on the floor. Someone stepped on it and crushed it with a shoe.

Another WHACK!

The White Woman fell flat on the ground, blood was streaming from her nose.

I was so confounded, it took me a couple of seconds to realize what was happening.

Jonathan grabbed me in his arms like I was the lightest of parcels, and started running.

I could hear car doors open and close. Men were shouting behind us. I figured they were helping the woman to her feet. I could still hear Spirit screaming from the back seat.

"Wait!" I cried. "Wait!"

Jonathan did not stop.

"We must go back!" I screamed. "We must get Spirit!"

He kept running.

The silver car was waiting, the back-seat door open. Jonathan threw me inside and jumped in. "DRIVE!" he shouted.

Rose pushed that gas pedal to the max as the car gave a huge roaming sound and bolted, screeching the floor as she did.

"Stop! Stop!" I cried. "We have to get Spirit!"

"We will, we will," Jonathan said, panting. "Outside of the parking lot… we'll think of something."

"You will *think* of something? When? It will be too late!"

"Sunny," he said, his face red and sweaty, "we will not leave her. Please trust us. We will not let her go back to Natures!"

I looked at him, confused. Why does it matter to them so much? Why should I trust him?

Rose was driving so fast through the parking lot, going up a spiral platform like we were strapped to a launched rocket, I felt dizzy.

The white car was right behind us, going as fast as we were going, screeching against the concrete floor, revving its engine.

Suddenly, Rose hit the break so hard, I flew onto the back of Jonathan's seat, biting my lip quite hard. I licked my lip and touched it with my hand. It was bleeding a little.

A shiny red car was lazily reversing back from its parking slot into the path. The driver, completely unaware of the frantic race that was coming his way like a rolling thunder, took his time, sliding into the path, almost completely blocking it.

Rose took a hard turn with the wheel. The silver car slid forward, zigzagging a little, avoiding the shiny red car only by a fraction. She kept going then stopped.

Behind us, the white car was not so lucky. A huge SMASH echoed in the parking lot. Wheels screeched very hard. Glass shattered. Engines were throttling, then muted.

Mayhem erupted. The driver of the shiny red car banged his head on the dashboard. He was holding his forehead in his hand like it was about to fall off. He pushed his way out of the car, staggering and raging. We could hear him scream such profanities I had not heard since the night at Emanuel Jessop's house. He grabbed a White Suit out of the white car, holding him by the collar, screaming.

That was my chance. I jumped out of the car.

"Sunny!" Jonathan shouted. "Sunny!"

I didn't listen. I ran back to where the red car and the white car were both standing impotently, one with a smashed front, the other a smashed side. The engine of the white car was smoking. I crept around the carnage site, quietly making my way to the backseat of the white car. The door was smashed open. Spirit was thrown on the back seat. She was unconscious.

There was no time for fear. No time for meticulous calculations. I had no time to think at all. I jumped in and grabbed her. The White Suit woman was slouched next to her on the back seat, still grabbing her nose in her hands. She reached out for me, her hand latching onto my hospital gown, I grabbed her hand in mine and peeled her off me. Her hand slid off. Spirit was so much heavier than I thought she would be, I could barely make a steady step with her in my arms. I was still so dizzy from lying for weeks on my hospital bed, and from the wild driving, that I was barely able to walk, let alone carry her too. Still, there was no other way. Step after step, walking as fast as I could, I rushed back to the silver car. I was still not entirely convinced about Jonathan and Rose, but they were certainly a safer bet than the White Suits.

The driver of the red car was still holding one of the White Suit, pinning him to the white car and screaming into his face, but another White Suite slid out of the white car and started running after me.

Gosh, Spirit was so heavy. Every step was a struggle. I could feel the pain in my right thigh, and the blood on my bitten lip. I didn't think I could make it. I didn't think I could carry her much further.

But I didn't need to. Jonathan came running. He grabbed Spirit from me and just shouted "RUN!"

We ran to the silver car. Rose's foot was waiting at the ready.

"Front seat!" Jonathan shouted.

I jumped into the front seat. Jonathan threw himself with Spirit onto the back seat, her head in his lap. Rose flattened the gas pedal and the car leaped forward.

She drove through the car park like a hurricane, until the exit gate was finally in sight. Rose slowed down and took a deep breath to calm herself.

The car slid close to the exit barrier. Rose waved her Nurse ID at the machine. A man in a dark blue uniform was sitting inside a booth, two barriers away from our lane. He gave us a faint polite smile. Rose smiled back nervously. The barrier lifted very slowly. Everything in this hospital was slow. Including recovery, I presumed. Behind us we could hear someone shouting, "Close that barrier! Don't let that car out!"

The facial expression of the man in the dark blue uniform changed from a polite smile to severe efficiency. He got up from his seat, left his little booth, and was making his way towards us very decisively.

"Ma'am?" he was talking to Rose. "I will need to see that ID again, Ma'am." He was knocking on her window with what looked like a flashlight. He pressed a security button on the machine near us, and the barrier was starting to close back down. "I will need you to step out of the car, Ma'am."

The barrier was closing. It was no more than one third down when Rose just hit the gas pedal with a considerable force. The car jumped forward, hitting the bottom of the barrier and breaking it off. The man started chasing us; two White Suits came out running from deep inside the parking lot and joined him. I could see them getting smaller as we drove off. They kept running for a while until they stopped.

33 PLANS CHANGE

"What do we do?" Rose asked anxiously. "We can't go to the house!"

"No. but we can't keep the data chip in them either. Wherever we go they will be onto us," Jonathan was checking Spirit as he spoke. He peeled her heavy eyelids and peered into her eyes.

"What do we do, Jonathan?"

"We must get to the beach house. We can be safe there. No one knows about the beach house." He took his glasses off and rubbed his eyes. "We have to stop at a motel on the way; we will need to do the procedure there."

"But…" Rose was confused.

"We have everything we need… we will keep it as sterile we can…."

Rose nodded.

"How is Spirit?" I asked, looking at them, my heart still aching.

"She'll be all right," he said. "She might be slightly concussed from the crash, but that is not why she is unconscious." He patted her hair very tenderly, which made me rather curious. "They have injected her with that serum, I have no doubt. She will regain consciousness fairly soon."

"Drive to the Seven Spades," he told Rose, and then he looked at me. "Sunny, we must take those chips out of you as soon as possible, because as long as they are still inside you, those nutters will be able to track you down no matter where we go." His eyes switched between me and Spirit, and back again. I thought they were kind. Sincere. Well meaning. "We were planning to have a little procedure, to take the chips out and do it in our clinic at home, but things got a little messy.... We discovered they were coming for you when they were already at the hospital reception downstairs. We only had three minutes to get you out." He was breathing very quickly. I bet that never in his entire life did he do something half this wild. He inhaled deeply. "We must have the procedure somewhere else… not the clinic… That means we have to be quick; local anesthesia may or may not be that effective with such a short time to prepare… so… it might uh, sting… a little."

"Just… a little?" I raised my eyebrows.

"Maybe more than a little," he corrected himself and smiled a little apologetic smile.

I nodded.

Rose was driving like mad.

"You can slow down a little, honey," he said and put his hand on the back of her left shoulder. "We don't want the Police to stop us."

She smiled at him through the front mirror and eased off the gas pedal.

I looked outside the window. The car was sailing through the streets, its reflection shining in silver through massive glass windows of towering office buildings. The city was buzzing with night life and seemed to be quite busy, twinkling in many colorful lights. People were sitting together, socializing in public dining rooms of all sorts. It reminded me of the community room at the farm.

"Do people normally eat together like that?" I wondered aloud.

"You mean, in restaurants?" Rose asked. "Well, yes. Sometimes. It's a nice thing to do."

I nodded.

I noticed that there was a rather astounding amount of trees and flowers everywhere, in small gardens and traffic islands. The city was so impressive, but I'd seen it before. I flew above it. I remembered.

We left the city center and were now driving through crummier streets, somehow more rundown and not as well kept. Trees and flowers became few and far between, until they disappeared completely and only buildings remained. There were less colorful restaurants and more small stores here and there and some deserted gas stations. Even the people who were walking outside or sitting on staircases were somehow more run down and not as well kept as those we passed celebrating in the city center. No one sleeps here, I thought.

Spirit started waking up from her slumber. Her eyes opened slowly, checking the car, looking up at Jonathan. She groaned.

"Hey you," I said to her from the front seat.

"Hey," she whispered. "Are you OK Sunny?"

"Yes," I smiled. "I'm OK."

"What happened?"

"Don't worry yourself too much, Spirit," Jonathan said softly. "You are in good hands now."

Rose maneuvered between streets, and then pulled into a car park behind an elongated, single level building. It was divided with dark doors every few meters, most doors were lit, except a few that weren't. Each door was numbered. At the far corner was a larger, glass double door with a sign that said "Office." The office was dark. There was an illuminated button at the door that said "Press here during afterhours." A sign on the door said "Vacancies." On top of the office corner was a bigger sign that must have been put there at least a hundred years ago, by the look of it. It was lit with a series of small lights all around it, and even so it was so faded, the writing was hard to decipher.

"Welcome to the Seven Spades Motel," Jonathan said. "Stay in the car until I get back."

34 THE SEVEN SPADES

Jonathan got to the office door and pressed the red illuminated button. Nothing happened. He turned his head back to us and shrugged awkwardly. He pressed the button again, several times.

The lights inside the office room switched on. The curtains were open, so we could see from the car that a man in a dark robe and thick grey hair was shuffling his feet to the door. He was coughing and spluttering into a handkerchief.

He opened the door only a smidgen.

"Yes?" The man welcomed Jonathan grumpily. The car windows were slightly down, the night air was crispy and clear, and I could hear that he had a loud, gurgling voice that did not sound all too friendly.

"I need a room for the night," Jonathan said.

"Now?"

"Yes," Jonathan hesitated. "It says here you have vacancies."

The man looked at him a little suspiciously, then cast his eyes on the car, then back at Jonathan. The car was dark; I don't think he could have seen us.

"You're a doctor?"

Jonathan patted his white suit, his Doctor's ID card still hanging around his neck. "Yes, yes I am."

"All right," the man said. "But no hanky panky in the room! I don't stand for that sort of thing!"

He opened the door wide, still looking suspiciously at the car.

Jonathan disappeared inside the office and was gone several long minutes. We were getting nervous waiting for him in the dark. Rose took a deep breath, I could hear her tapping her foot nervously, which made *me* nervous too.

Finally, the office's door opened and Jonathan returned. "Room number eight," he said.

Rose started the engine again and reversed the car until we were aligned with door number eight. Jonathan jumped out and opened the room with the key he'd brought from the office.

Spirit and I rushed inside while Jonathan and Rose opened the car boot and took out bags and all sorts of equipment. They were setting everything up in the center of the room. Rose drew the curtains closed.

The room was plain. It had a single bed and a small table with two chairs. Everything was beige with touches of what, to my horror, seemed to be a kind of peach shade, although somewhat faded. The carpet was a little burnt in places, and was in desperate need of a wash. Everything smelt funny. Moldy.

I'd only just got out of the hospital, but I realized that the most important medical procedure of my life was going to take place right then, in that shabby room.

"We are all set," Rose announced.

"OK girls," Jonathan sounded all purposeful, "We will inject you both with the local anesthesia at the same time. The one who goes first will probably feel more pain, as it takes longer to set. You may have numb fingers for a while, and it might sting... more than a little."

"I'll go first," I said.

They put a cold gel on our wrists and with a hand-held scanner located our chips. They were tiny. They marked the spot with a pen on our skins and then jabbed us deeply with a very long needle, inserting the local anesthetics. The needle going in was in itself an unpleasant experience, but we'd been through worse pain before. Spirit winced as the needle went in again and again.

Then it was time to cut through the skin and pull the chip out. They poured some brown and smelly liquid on my wrist. Rose handed me a clean, rolled towel. "Bite this if it gets too much," she said.

I wasn't sure whether to look or to avert my eyes from my hand. What might make the pain more tolerable? In the end the pain was such that I just had to close my eyes and bite hard into the towel. I would even say that the anesthetic did not even begin to kick in as they dived through with their forceps and their fine collection of small knives. But it was very quick. By the time I dared to open my eyes again, Rose was already stitching me up. "Two stitches are all we need" she said. She put a white cream on top and then a small bandage. The chip they threw into a glass of water.

"Congratulations, Sunny," Jonathan said. "You are no longer the marked property of Natures Farms."

I can't put into words how that made me feel. I was still quite confused about the whole situation. The suspicion I harbored for Jonathan and Rose was fading very quickly. Not only did they not turn us over to the White Suits, they'd just liberated me from being so easily trackable by Natures. Maybe now I could really be just a normal girl? Just a girl. Maybe I could stop running. No more running. That thought in itself made me feel relieved and hopeful.

Rose hugged me, but there was no time to rejoice; it was Spirit's turn to undergo her procedure now.

In no time at all the entire ordeal was behind us. Two chips were sunk into the glass. We were truly free. Free of the farm. Free of the

White Suits. Free of the fear and the pain.

"They might still be able to track us this far," Jonathan interrupted my elation. "We have to get going right away."

They packed everything as quickly as they had unpacked. Blood soaked towels were carefully placed in a rubbish bag and put into the car boot. Rose wiped the table clean. All evidence of what had just happened there was gone. The chips were flushed into the toilet, the glass was washed.

Jonathan left the key on the table and switched off the lights.

We rushed out of the room and into the car.

"To the beach house then?" Rose asked.

"Yes."

She smiled.

We all smiled.

The silver car pulled out of the parking next to door number eight. We were about to leave the Seven Spades, taking the dark turn that lead out of the driveway, when Jonathan said with urgency, "Wait! Pull over behind that black car there, and kill the engine, Rose!"

Rose followed his instructions. She turned off the engine and switched off the headlights.

"What is it?" she whispered.

Jonathan did not even answer. A white car just passed us, slowly making its way towards the office of the Seven Spades.

35 INTO THE NIGHT

We watched the white car stop outside of the office. The white car's engine had been turned off and a man got out. He approached the office door.

We watched as the man in the dark robe and the thick grey hair opened the office door. He did not look pleased. The men were talking.

"Now," Jonathan said.

Rose turned on the car's engine, keeping the lights off. We could see the men turn their heads towards the sound of our car driving off. The silver car slid back into the night.

My heart was beating very fast. How soon before the white car would be right behind us again?

We were back on the main road. Rose turned the headlights back on. She was driving fast but confidently. Turn after turn lead us into a web of narrow streets. I kept turning my head around nervously, but there was no white car behind us.

"Can you see them?" Rose asked.

"No," I replied.

Finally, when I was getting quite certain that we'd lost the white car, relief washed over me, and it was so overwhelming, so overpowering, I could just as well be floating. I looked at Rose and Jonathan, his hand was on her thigh. Did these people truly just get into possible trouble with the law, putting their jobs on the line, just in order to help Spirit and me? To free us from Natures' claws? It seemed as if they did just that. I couldn't understand why, but I was thankful.

"Thank you Rose and Jonathan" I said to them from the back seat.

They nodded and smiled, "You are very welcome."

We left the city. Darkness ensued, only the headlights of passing cars lit the night. We seemed to be driving through more and more of those plains where nothing grew.

Rose turned the radio on. Soft music filled the car. At the farm we listened to very little music. We had an old music player that was probably already outdated by the time I was born. The musical collection it could play was very limited, and at some point, we just got fed up with listening to the same music and the same songs over and over and over again. Mom used to sing to me when I was little. She had a lovely voice. I missed her.

I let the music and the darkness and the joy and the relief engulf me, and sweet sleep found me. I don't think I dreamt.

When I woke, music was no longer playing. The car was silent but for the soft humming noise of the engine. The sky was the color of light grey, with kisses of soft pink. Tall grass and all sort of brushy weeds covered the side of the road, which was white and sandy. Beyond them was a massive clifftop, and beyond it – was the sea. Dark grey and foamy, waves splattering and playful. I had never seen the sea before. It was the most beautiful scene that I had ever seen. I could hardly contain my excitement.

"Good morning," Rose's warm voice and kind smile welcomed me softly, "ever seen the sea before?"

I smiled back and shook my head.

"It is beautiful, isn't it?"

"It is amazing."

"Here, you need to smell it too," she said and pressed a button at her side. My window slid all the way down, allowing the cool morning breeze to bring the salty, peaty sea air to me, to dance around me, to caress my face, to blow my hair. It was such a powerful experience I had to just close my eyes and succumb to it completely.

"Oh, sweet Mercy, is that the sea?" Spirit awoke, shrieking with excitement. "It is absolutely glorious," she said, while breathing in the sea air deeply.

"We might be able to swim in it when we get to the beach house," Rose said. We shrieked again, uncontrollably, and woke Jonathan.

"At the sea already eh?" he said, and stretched as much as he was able. "How fast were you going darling? Bank Robbery or Old Retirement Village?" From his tone it was clear he was teasing her.

Rose laughed. "Neither!"

If I could touch that moment, free and unmarked, the four of us in that car, the sea so close to us, the salty breeze all around us... I would have touched happiness.

36 THE BEACH HOUSE

The road departed from the cliff and the sea, but Rose promised us that we would meet the sea again, when we got to where their beach house stood. The tall brushy weeds and long grass kept following us on our way. Rose turned the radio back on. There was no music, but a monotone voice was talking.

"And now to local news. A burglary took place last night at the Central Hospital. Two female Farm assets were taken from their hospital beds. The thieves are suspected to be Doctor Jonathan Appledorn, and his accomplice, wife Rose, a nurse at the hospital. The stolen goods are said to have been an investment of Natures Farms. The suspects' license plate is…."

Rose turned the radio off abruptly. Heavy silence lingered.

"They can't find us now without your chips," Jonathan said, "no one knows about the beach house."

"No one except Violet," Rose corrected him.

"Violet would be completely on our side."

"Yes, that is true," she said, then added very nervously, "They have our license plate number."

"We'll park our car under the car port and cover it. We have good old Griselda there. She will do us just fine."

"I suppose," Rose sighed.

"You may as well go Bank Robbery now darling," Jonathan said, and Rose pressed hard on the gas pedal.

A long, white, gravel side road stretched along a pretty cove and finally brought us to the beach house. It was an impressive cottage made of beautiful dark wood. It was remote, standing on its own windswept beach. The sea was a very short distance away. Rose parked the silver car under the open car port next to an old looking, but very clean and nicely maintained car.

We all got out of the car.

"Hello Griselda, old girl!" Jonathan said. He was talking to the other car. I had to laugh.

The front door of the beach house was huge and wooden with a large silvery handle. Rose opened the door for us and allowed us to walk in first.

"Welcome home," she said.

They were the most beautiful two words I could ever have wished to hear.

It was a spacious, airy, single story house. Large windows everywhere overlooked the sea. The kitchen, the dining area and the living room were all combined into a single open space, the sea providing the most beautiful focal point from every corner. There were also large sliding doors that lead out to an expansive wooden deck, surrounded by the glistening sand, the brushy weeds and the grass. A large, massive, open wood burner took a great share of the opposite wall, and beyond it, a couple of small wide steps led to a slightly lower level of the house, where a wide sitting room led to the bedrooms. There were four bedrooms in the house. One of them was Rose and Jonathan's main bedroom. It had its own bathroom and toilet. Another room was used as an office. It had medical equipment, medical books and all that they needed for their practice. The other two rooms were supposedly for us, each of us to our own room, but we were reluctant to separate. All the rooms were beautifully made, tastefully decorated and welcoming.

"Don't worry, you don't need to separate. This room can easily contain two beds, we'll just move the bed from the other bedroom here," Rose reassured us.

We went back to the kitchen, where Jonathan was making pancakes. "Prepare to be amazed!" he said and winked to us. "My pancakes are just what the doctor has ordered!"

Spirit giggled.

I walked around, getting more familiar with the house. We were so lucky. This was simply heaven.

I came by a shelf that displayed lots of photographs held in pretty frames. I recognized Rose and Jonathan, even when they were younger they were quite a lovely couple, Rose with her pretty blonde hair and Jonathan with his bright, blue eyes. There were other people in some of the photographs, possibly family members or friends. And there was a girl. She was in almost all of the photographs. As a baby in one, a toddler in the other, driving a trike in another with Rose laughing beside her, on Jonathan's shoulders holding a balloon, blowing five candles on a birthday cake with Jonathan blowing too, behind her back.

I took the largest photograph into my hand and stared at it. The frame was elaborate, golden, and extremely heavy. A beautiful girl with blonde hair done in two plaits, large blue eyes, about eight or nine years old, was smiling at me from the photograph. It was the same girl.

I immediately realized that the most burning question of all, "Why?" was answered right there on that shelf.

"Her name was Arabella," Rose said softly behind me. "She was the joy of our lives. The most beautiful, happy, loving... stubborn little child." She smiled sadly.

"What happened to her?"

"She got ill… five years ago… we couldn't save her," Rose's eyes teared up.

"I am so sorry."

"We believe you two are the new beginning that we've craved for, for so long," she said, wiping her tears away. "The Sweet Mercy brought you to us."

I smiled.

Suddenly I felt her hand patting my hair… the way Mom would do. It was nice. I missed it so much.

"You need to rest up Sunny. Your shot wound has not fully healed yet. Once you are stronger I'll take you to the nearest village where we can get some new clothes for you and Spirit."

We ate Jonathan's oat pancakes drizzled with maple syrup and drank glasses of almond milk.

"So… are you amazed?" he asked, very pleased with himself.

"Yes," we giggled. We were amazed.

The day warmed up. Rose opened the sliding doors to the deck.

"Let's dip those little feet in the sea!" Jonathan suggested.

We ran outside screaming and shrieking, skipping and dancing. We had so much excitement built up inside us we weren't quite sure how to let it out. It was quite the show.

Approaching the sea was like approaching a live mythological beast. Waves kept chasing us out, then withdrawing back in. The water was cold and ticklish. I soaked my feet to the knees, being pushed and pounded by the waves, surrounded with white foam. I ran out and dug my feet into the wet sand. The sand felt warm on my toes. It was magical.

Later we sat outside on the deck on deep beach chairs under a wide shading umbrella, sipping lemonade, inhaling the sea air and solving crossroads together.

Suddenly the phone rang inside. We all jumped. It was a loud, angry, anxious ring.

"Only one person on this planet has this number," Jonathan said to Rose.

"Oh, please darling… can you pick up and tell her I am asleep or something?"

"You know your sister can read me like an open book," Jonathan objected.

"Yes… she has that ability with everyone," Rose added and went inside. She picked up the noisy phone. "Hello Violet."

She walked to the office to continue the conversation from there.

When she got back outside her face was darker.

"Everything all right?" Jonathan asked.

"Yes… yes," she said. Clearly it wasn't. Even I could pick that up.

Evening came; I chose a book from the library and was reading on the puffy sofa. Spirit was drawing a picture at the table.

Rose brought us towels and night gowns. We washed and changed, in turn. There was no fear this time. There was no monster lurking at the door. It was such a liberating new experience.

Our bedroom was reorganized to have both beds side by side, with a beautiful small night table between them. Rose drew the curtains; they were the color of cream and gold. Jonathan came to say good night. They were both standing at the door, hugging each other, smiling.

In the darkened room, just before I closed my eyes, Spirit said, "Sunny?"

"Yes?"

"I'm happy."

"I'm happy too."

37 HAPPINESS

I woke up from a dreamless night. For a second I wasn't quite sure where I was. The curtains were still drawn together and the room was still dark. For a split-second fear filled my heart and jumped into my throat, but with memory and recognition came peacefulness. I could hear Spirit breathing calmly in the bed next to me. Beyond the warmth and coziness of the room I could even hear the sound of the waves, crushing playfully onto the beach, chasing each other over and over in an endless perpetual game. It was serene. I stayed in bed for a while longer, just enjoying the sense of comfort and calm, soaking the tranquility, then got up and made my way to the kitchen. I passed the study room where Jonathan was sitting and writing.

"Good morning," I said through the open door.

He jumped up of his seat and came to me. "Good morning Sunny," he smiled, "how did you sleep?"

"Very well, thank you."

"That's very good. Nothing like the sea air to make you feel all better eh?"

I nodded, smiling.

"Let me take a look at your hand," he said, and checked the stitches. "Jolly good," he said. "In a few days we'll remove the stitches and it will be as good as gold."

He replaced the bandage and sent me off to the kitchen. "I believe Rose is making an attempt at baking," he said with a chuckle… "Sweet Mercy."

I laughed.

The kitchen bench top was covered with all sorts of ingredients; flour was spread everywhere, peeled bananas and pitted dated were laid on a plate, a bag of brown sugar stood amidst the mess, its top open wide, as an open mouth waiting to be fed. Rose was wearing an apron; it was dusted with flour. She was peering at a recipe book as she noticed me. She welcomed me with a big hug and kissed my forehead. It was nice.

"How did you sleep?"

"Very well, thank you."

"Hungry?"

I nodded.

"Please just help yourself to anything you find, bread is over there, the fruit bowl over there, you'll find muesli in the pantry, and the fridge is full of stuff. Just grab whatever you want Sunny. This is your house."

I smiled.

"I'll make us a cup of tea. I need a break from trying to figure out this recipe," she said with a sigh. I giggled.

I took two slices of the grainy bread and put them in the toaster. Then I helped myself to a shiny red apple, washed and sliced it thinly. I opened the fridge door. It was indeed full of so much stuff I found it hard to choose what to get. I settled on the smoked cashew spread when my eyes fell on a round item, wrapped in a colorful wrap. I grabbed it and held it in my hands. I recognized the wrapping. What it said. What it stood for. The wrapping was colorful and pretty. It had a picture of a woman with a young girl, both smiling. 'Natures. The REAL taste of Cheese.' There, within this round, cold, wrapped cheese, with its stupid wrapping and grotesquely happy picture, all of my life's pains and sorrows were concentrated. My hands started shaking and the tears started to overflow. In front of me I could see Mom and her dead sons, I could see Precious, Antim, Freckles, Alberta, Dawn, and above all Rosichi... all the agony, all the misery... for this. The cheese dropped out of my hands and onto the floor.

Rose finally realized what was happening.

"Oh no… oh no… oh no!" she rushed to me. "I'm so sorry! I'm so sorry Sunny! I wasn't even thinking… I…. we… we stopped with the milk a while ago, only the cheese… To tell you the truth I think they make it deliberately addictive… I found it so hard to give it up… until now I mean, with you and Spirit… I just… I didn't… I didn't connect the dots. I am so sorry Sunny. It is gone now. We will never ever have any of that rubbish again."

She picked up the round cheese and threw it in the bin. Her arms were wrapped around me again, I could hear her quickened breathing breaking. "Please, forgive me." Slowly I put my arms around her too. I suppose even good people can be fooled by colorful packaging and clever lies.

We stood there like that for a while until Spirit walked in, still yawning and rubbing her eyes. She ran to us, half skipping, and stretched her arms around both of us, making it into a three-way hug.

"Shall we bake a cake?" Rose asked

"Oh yes! With lots of frosting!" Spirit answered excitedly.

We spend the morning in the kitchen, baking a cake and some mushroom muffins. The smells that came out of the oven were divine.

Rose gave me a dress to wear, from her own closet. It fitted me perfectly. It was so beautiful, light blue with big white flowers. I couldn't stop swooshing it from side to side. Spirit already had a small collection of dresses that Rose gave her while she was recovering in hospital and I was still in and out of La La Land. Then she combed Spirit's hair and plaited it.

"Would you like me to brush your hair, Sunny?" Rose asked.

I'd never had anyone brush my hair. Maybe Mom, but even that was such a long time ago I couldn't remember. I said yes. I enjoyed the attention, the pampering, the connection, the obvious fondness. I only started to realize then how much I craved it. How nice it was.

Rose combed my hair gently. "What a beautiful hair you have, Sunny," she said. Then she made it up into a tail.

"Wow," Spirit said, "you look so nice."

I did too.

I was happy.

38 THE LITTLE BEACH VILLAGE

All that sudden, happiness made me think of Rosichi. I missed her a lot. I missed her laughter, her sense of mischievousness... The way we used to sneak into each other's room after nightfall, hide under the covers, gossip and giggle about stuff that happened at the farm. How she would always let me have the biggest slice of any pie she'd bake, and even when it was choke-on-this terrible, I used to tell her it was the best pie I'd ever had... I remembered the night we went looking after her mother... the night I got my first peek into The Shed. After Rosichi's mom's disappearance, I felt it was my duty to look after her. I felt it was my job to mend every insult, every disappointment, every hurtful encounter. But in the end, I failed to mend the worst hurtful encounter of them all... I wished I could turn back time. I missed my best friend. My confidante. She would have loved it there, at the beach house, I was sure of it. She would have loved running on the white beach, tipping her toes in the cool water. She would have liked Rose and Jonathan too. I kept wondering, if she hadn't done it... if she hadn't touched the fence... would she be alive with us? Could we have raised her baby together, as a family?

Family. My beautiful sister, Antim. She was almost three. Antim would have loved it there too. How she would have loved the beach. What was I going to do about her still being stuck in the farm? The thought of her in the hands of Natures' sadists made me restless. I failed with Rosichi, I couldn't fail with Antim, but I had no idea what to do. I was still figuring out my own story.

That afternoon Jonathan taught us how to fly a kite. The wind was sufficient to get it flying, he thought. We spent a good hour running up and down on the beach. I nearly couldn't feel my healing gunshot wound any more. The stitches were out and the flesh was almost mended. We giggled and laughed. Jonathan wasn't really that good at flying kites, to tell you the truth, but we overlooked it.

There was only a minor hiccup, really it was not a big deal all considering, when Jonathan called Spirit Arabella. It was a slip of a tongue and he quickly corrected himself and apologized. I don't think Spirit minded.

We were having a late snack on the deck when the phone rang again. It made everyone jump.

"I guess I should take that," Rose said.

She went to the office and picked up the phone.

I suddenly had a very strong urge to listen in. I knew that after the previous conversation with her sister, Rose came back to us and she was not happy. I felt a need to know. I had a strong sense this had to do with us.

I excused myself to go to the bathroom. The office door was open. I could hear Rose speaking in her warm voice.

"It's too soon, Violet…"

"I know you mean well, but it's too soon…"

"We are fine. No one knows about the beach house…"

"You worry for no reason, Violet…. "

"No. I already told you, it is too soon…"

"I don't know when will be the right time. Not now…"

I continued to the bathroom, not to cause suspicion. By the time I returned, Rose was already back outside again. They were all running like mad trying to get the kite soaring, laughing.

I spent the evening reading my book. Spirit was listening to some music. Jonathan and Rose were sitting outside, talking. Bits of conversation drifted through the door, and between the music notes, and reached me.

"She worries for our safety," Rose said. "She thinks they are perfectly capable of locating us here."

Jonathan sounded a lot more confident, saying something like, "Rubbish" and, "Your sister is too involved," and other bits I couldn't quite understand, and then, "Why don't you just ask Sunny?"

That got my ears peeled, but not much else was said.

That night, Spirit had a nightmare. She was battling demons in her sleep and it woke me up. She never had bad dreams while we were running, too focused on surviving. But now that life had sort of settled around us, her dreams were catching up. I sat on her bed and stroked her hair and her face until the demons went away and she was breathing softly and peacefully.

I looked at her cute, brave face, wondering how badly messed up we were. Would we ever be just normal children? Was it even possible?

I was tired at breakfast. I didn't manage to fall back to sleep for hours after Spirit's nightmare.

"Are you OK?" Jonathan wondered.

I nodded. "I'm just a little bit tired," I said.

He smiled. "Sea air will do that to you eh?"

Everything was about the sea air with Jonathan.

Rose suggested we go to the nearest village and get some new clothes. It sounded like fun but I was a bit nervous. I loved the peaceful solitude of the beach house, how far from danger and from other people it seemed to be. Leaving it, even if only for a short time, scared me. Spirit was very excited about going. We wore light cardigans to hide the stitches on our wrists. Rose also gave us wide rimmed sun hats that shaded our faces and hid us rather well. She put on a large pair of sunglasses and a large sun hat and off we went on our jolly way, riding Griselda the old girl…

Griselda was not as comfortable as the silver car was. Every small bump on the road made us bounce high. She was also so loud we couldn't really hear anything else, so talking was out, and also music. We rolled our windows down and let Jonathan's sea air fill the car and our lungs, blow our hair and tear our eyes. The long, white gravel side road twisted and turned this way and that way, until finally we joined a slightly wider road that later joined the main road. I was relieved. I couldn't stand the bouncing. I was feeling my gunshot wound again, after I almost managed to completely forget it ever existed.

We did not have far to go. The first exit to yet another small road came only a few miles away.

The small village was neat. You could tell it was close to the sea by the amount of boats, kites, swimwear, diving gear and surf boards everywhere. All the houses were small and freshly painted. They all had pots of flowers all around them, including flower baskets hanging at entrances and all through the main road.

An alley of small, nicely decorated shops and a little supermarket was pretty much all there was to the shopping experience.

Rose parked the car. We rolled our windows back up. Before we left

Griselda, Rose said, "Girls, while we are here, call me Joan... we don't want to cause suspicion."

We decided to first go into one of the more centrally-located shops. It had some nice dresses displayed on mannequins at its window. A doorbell that hung over the door rang as we walked in. Inside, the shop smelled a little stuffy. A large fan was sifting the air from the ceiling. A woman with large glasses and a bright purple lipstick stood at the counter, reading.

"Good morning," she said, "what would you be after?"

"Good morning. A few dresses and shorts for the girls, some shoes and socks."

"Sure, we have the lot," the woman said.

We walked around the shop picking items, looking at others, taking things off hangers then putting them back on again. The woman's eyes were fixed on us all along. Her stare passed from me to Spirit to Rose and back again.

I selected a couple of dresses to wear, also a pair of shorts and a couple of shirts. The shoes were all simple canvas shoes. I picked a black pair and several pairs of socks.

As I went to the only fitting room in the shop I took my hat off. Inside the fitting room, which was only a tiny space separated from the rest of the shop with a curtain that looked more like a sheet, I tried on the clothes. They fitted me well. I was so pleased seeing myself in the mirror wearing pretty dresses and comfortable new shoes, looking well, happy, that I forgot everything else. I casually drew the curtain to the changing room wide open. So taken with joy, I carelessly uttered "Rose, these clothes are simply wonderful!"

Rose. I said Rose.

Across the room I could clearly see Rose looking very pale. I could see that even through her sun glasses. Next to her, Spirit was looking at me with wild eyes, indicating something to me with the mildest of gestures. I couldn't quite decipher what she wanted me to do. She was asking me something, without words.

What was it?

I stood there, still in the fitting room, curtain wide open, bewildered.

Spirit was pale and shaken. What did she want me to do?

I looked from her to Rose whose mouth was tightly shut together. She was nervous. From Rose to the shop keeper who was looking at me intently. Suspiciously.

"Is everything OK darling?" the shop keeper asked in her nonchalant tone.

What was I supposed to answer? A minute ago, I was on top of the world, admiring my reflection in the mirror, now, thrown back to a world of fear and confusion.

A figure crossed the shop's front window. At first, I didn't pay much attention, only capturing her in the corner of my eye like a meaningless, passing shadow, nearly missing it. But something from deep in my subconscious mind was screaming at me to pay attention immediately. The figure, tall and svelte, the hair short and dark, sleek and combed to one side, had paused. Her clothes were white. Like an electric shock, realization of who might be standing right outside the door made me sweat buckets in cold terror, soaking the back of the new dress.

The figure hesitated. Her head was turning towards the window, looking into the shop.

Get back inside! That was what Spirit was telling me. That was what my brain was now screaming to me. Get back inside!

I think I squeaked. With a single move I drew the sheet closed and ducked against the inner wall. Did she see me? Did she notice me?

I cuddled my knees together to stop them from shaking.

The bell that hung above the door rang cheerfully. I could hear my breath and it seemed as loud as a hurricane. The large fan on the wall was going around and around and around.

"Good morning," the shop keeper said.

"Good morning," responded the woman who had just entered the shop. I knew that voice. I could recognize it anywhere. The White Suit woman. The perpetrator of my worst nightmares.

"What would you be after?"

"Something special," the White Suit woman responded, her words slowly and potently articulated.

"Special…. Like for a special occasion?" the shop keeper wondered.

The White Suit woman did not respond. I could tell by the way her footsteps echoed in the store that she was walking around. That she has turned towards Rose.

"Lovely morning isn't it?" The White Woman said.

"Yes, very nice," Rose responded, her voice sounding different. Deeper somehow, and with a foreign accent. I could hear she was pushing hangers around nervously, like she was trying to pretend to be looking for clothes.

A pause ensued. It seemed to go on forever.

The large fan on the wall was going around and around and around.

"Are you from around here?" The White Suit woman asked.

"No, just passing," the fake Rose answered, trying to sound very casual. I did not think she sounded convincing at all. "Tourist," she added.

"Would you be after a dress?" the shopkeeper asked the White Suit woman.

There was no response. Only echoes of footsteps approaching the fitting room.

I could see her shadow now, falling on the sheet. The tip of her shoes peaked under the edge. Her hand was reaching to the curtain. There was nowhere to hide. I was crouched by the wall, hugging my knees, holding my breath. There was no escape.

"Are you going to try something on?" a nervous, foreign-accented, deeper-voiced-than-usual Rose was asking.

The shadow turned away from the curtain.

"I want to try on this dress, and this is the only fitting room."

Slowly, the White Suit woman stepped further away from the curtain.

Rose drew a very narrow gap in the curtain and slithered inside quickly, closing it behind her. She looked at me, her face red and glistening with sweat, lips quivering. Her finger went to her lips signaling silence.

Where was Spirit?

The footsteps echoed away from the fitting room.

"Have you seen anyone suspicious today?" the White Suit woman asked the shop keeper.

"Apart from you?" the shop keeper was trying to be smart. The White Suit woman did not like that at all. Her voice was very cold when she responded.

"On the poster behind you there are photos of criminals that we are looking for… Have you even bothered looking at it?"

"Those posters change all the time, it's hard to keep up," the shop keeper said.

"Well, please take a good look. These people are dangerous. We received a tip-off, suggesting that they might be hiding in this village somewhere."

The shop keeper did not respond.

"There is a nice reward for their capture," The White Suit woman added. "Surely you could do with some money, couldn't you?" I could almost hear the wicked smile in her voice.

Silence befell the shop. Rose was pretending to be trying on the dress.

The White Suit woman was searching inside her pockets.

"This is my card. If you come across any of those criminals, please call my number directly."

"Not the police?" the shop keeper seemed confused.

"AND the police."

There was a long pause.

The large fan on the wall was going around and around and around.

We could hear footsteps drifting further away from us. The doorbell rang as the door opened and then again as it was shut.

Rose tossed the dress she pretended to try on away and let out a deep sigh. I got up on my feet, my hands and my back sticky with sweat. We waited a few moments before slowly, tentatively, coming out of the fitting room. Spirit crawled from under a clothes rack.

 The shop keeper looked at us suspiciously, saying nothing, the White Suit woman's card in her hand.

"Well, I suppose we can just pay now," Rose said quickly.

"Won't the other one be trying her clothes on first?"

"No, no. We took the right size," Rose said, a little nervously.

The woman took her time calculating the total. She glanced at Rose over and over again; when she wasn't calculating or glancing at Rose, she was glancing at the black phone beside her on the counter, or the card she was still holding in her hand.

The large fan on the wall was going around and around and around.

Behind the counter, on the wall, there was a poster. My face was on it. Also, Spirit's and Rose's and Jonathan's. The title said "REWARD!" and underneath it, "HAVE YOU SEEN THESE PEOPLE?" It said, "Call the Police".

I quickly put my hat back on.

Rose was becoming extremely restless. She just took out a 200 bill and put it nervously on the counter.

"I'm sure that would be enough to cover everything," she said.

The woman stared.

The large fan on the wall was going around and around and around.

We picked up everything and rushed out of the door. The bell rang behind us.

We walked very fast on the pavement. There were people everywhere now. They were all looking at us, or at least that was the feeling I had. Everyone was looking at us.

Was the White Suit woman still there? Was she looking at us? We started running. We ran to Griselda. The old girl was not very happy. It took a few attempts to get her started. The woman stepped out of the shop, watching us, the card still in her hand.

Finally, Griselda obliged and her engine roared. We turned around and drove off, as fast as Griselda would allow, which wasn't very fast at all. All the while the woman was watching.

39 SISTERS ACT

None of us uttered a single word all the way back to the beach house, and not because of Griselda's loud engine masking our speech, but because we were too distraught to talk.

We were so close to being captured again, it was surreal.

A depressing thought kept troubling me. Even here, in the peaceful beach house, with these people who clearly cared for us and wanted to help us, danger was everywhere. We would never be completely free. Not anywhere.

The phone rang again in the evening while Rose and Jonathan were sitting on the deck, Spirit and I inside. Rose had been in the office for a rather long time. She returned troubled.

"Everything OK dear?"

"Violet wasn't happy about our little adventure this morning," she said. "She thinks I took an unnecessary risk."

Jonathan didn't say things like "Rubbish" or "Your sister is too involved" this time. He wasn't happy about what happened in the village; in fact, he was troubled by it as well. I don't think they realized quite how persistent Natures would be in trying to find us.

"She still wants to come here."

"You know what I think you should do," Jonathan said and nodded towards the house.

Rose looked inside and nodded. She came inside and sat next to me on the puffy sofa. I closed my book and waited.

"Sunny, those phone calls we are getting every day, are all from my sister, Violet. She is the only other person in the world who knows about the beach house, and has the number."

I nodded.

"We were always very close, Violet and I. As little girls and even now. I trust her completely."

I nodded again.

"Violet… she is a very strong person. She is very… disciplined. Her views of the world are very firmly set, so to speak."

I had no idea what she was trying to say, but I sensed that whatever it was, it hadn't been said yet, so I nodded.

"The things that she deems wrong, she would object to with all her heart, and she would... fight against it. If she considers something an injustice, she would fight against it... to fix it. She sighed. "Like what Natures are doing on their farms... on your farm for example... this whole business of dairy slavery... she... she fights against it, with a group of people like her. They are *activists*."

"Like you and Jonathan?"

Rose laughed. "Oh... hardly... we are not really..."

"But you rescued us."

"That was almost unintentional... I mean... we just fell in love with the both of you... It wasn't planned... We are not the sort of people who dedicate every minute of every day to fight against it... We sort of, fell into it..." She gave it a bit more thought. "Maybe we are becoming a bit more like activists, just by the sheer fact that we rescued you and we would never give you away... But... Violet, she is a high-ranking member of DaSLiF, the Dairy Slaves Liberation Front. It's an organization of activists dedicated to bringing down the industry. For them the ethical fight is what they live for."

I was amazed. I had no idea that there were people who were fighting for us. Dedicating their lives to it. All this time, we were not alone?

"Violet asked to meet you, Sunny," Rose said. "She's been asking it for a while now, even when you were still in hospital... I kept pushing it off. But now I think, maybe it should be your decision... Would you like to meet her?"

I didn't need to think twice.

"Yes."

40 THE DREAM

Rose called Violet back. A meeting was set for the next day in the afternoon.

That night I dreamt again. I hadn't had any dreams in a while, so this one almost took me by surprise, even while dreaming.

I was at the beach house, in the living room, reading on the sofa. I sort of realized this was a dream. Something made me drop my book and go outside to the deck. Everything looked the same except for one thing, my mom was standing there. She was right at the edge of the deck, her back to me. Her hair was waving in the light breeze. She was still tinted in gold, exuding light, as if she'd swallowed the sun. She was watching something. She was watching the road leading to the house, which you could observe from that point on the deck.

"Mom?" I was so happy to see her. I missed her so much. I ran to her, my arms reaching, I tried to touch her, but my hand went right through.

"Mom?"

She didn't hear me. She did not turn towards me. She just stood there, watching. I came to stand by her. I looked at her from the side. She was so beautiful, so tall and so very commanding. I watched the road with her, wondering what she was looking for. We stood there, very still, side by side.

"I love you Mom," I whispered. "I miss you."

She did not hear me. She did not move her eyes from the road.

Something was approaching. A car. A white car.

'Perhaps it's Violet?' I thought to myself in my dream.

But the car was white like the one in the hospital parking lot, and my heart started to beat rather quickly. Just before the car disappeared out of view from where we stood, I caught a good glimpse of the person driving it. It was the White Suit woman.

They were coming.

I panicked. I wanted to run inside the house and warn everyone, but my legs became like jelly, sticky and unyielding. I tried to scream, but no voice came out. The doorbell rang.

From my position on the deck I looked into the house and I saw Jonathan at the door. He opened it. They were talking. The woman reached into her pocket and took something out.

266

A gun. She had a gun. She pointed it at Jonathan. He took a step in.

I could hear the gun shot like it was fired right next to my head. I saw Jonathan falling to the floor. He had a bloodstain right where his heart was. And it was growing, widening, soaking his shirt.

"Jonathan! Jonathan!" I screamed. No voice came out of me. I could see the White Suit woman taking a big step over Jonathan's body, and going towards the bedrooms. She disappeared from my sight.

I couldn't move, I couldn't run. I just stood there, screaming in silence.

"Sunny!" my mom snapped at me.

I turned to her. She was looking directly at me. The sun inside her eyes burning.

"*Jonathan,*" she said.

"*Jonathan.*"

I woke up panting, sweating and in tears. I knew what I needed to do.

41 THE VISIT

Nervousness and tension were in the air all morning. We each were absorbed in our own little world. I picked up a new book but while my eyes followed the words my mind was not picking up anything. It was somewhere else completely. I could sense the metallic taste of fear in my throat again, the hollowness in the stomach. The dread.

Tick, tick, tick, the minutes passed, one chasing the other. We had a small lunch. No one seemed to be particularly hungry.

It was approaching two o'clock in the afternoon when a car could be seen far away on the gravel road, approaching the house.

Rose was preparing some refreshments in the kitchen. Jonathan was watching out the window close to the entrance.

"What type of car does your sister drive these days, honey, do you know?"

"I have no idea," she said, ripping a bag of salted chickpeas and tipping it into a bowl.

"Would it be white, do you think?"

"White? No. It would certainly *not* be white," Rose said, then chuckled, "My sister would not be caught *dead* in a white car like those people she detests..." and suddenly she stopped what she was doing and went to the window. They stood there staring, when Rose let go of a little nervous yelp. The car was white.

"Take the girls and hide!" Jonathan said firmly.

"But... what..."

"Rose, just do it! Take Spirit and Sunny and hide! NOW!"

We ran after her to the main bedroom and into the walk-in closet where we cowered together. As a hiding place it was really no good. They would be onto us in two seconds. If they managed to find us here at the beach house, a walk-in wardrobe was not what was going to stop them. Spirit was crying, Rose was shaking. I was the only one still functioning.

The doorbell rang.

Jonathan sure took his time answering that door. It rang again.

We could hear him turning the key. It echoed in the silent house like a thousand heartbeats.

"Yes?" he said.

"Mr. Appledorn, you are a difficult man to find," said the other voice. I knew that voice. Dull and arrogant, purposeful and loathsome. The White Suit woman.

"Do I know you?"

"Let's skip the pleasantries Mr Appledorn," she said. "I believe you have something that belongs to me."

"I have no idea what you are talking about lady… If you have any claims against me, I suggest you get a search warrant from the police."

"Now, now, Mr Appledorn. I truly do not believe involving the police and all the red tape is necessary. You and I both know you and your wife are harboring two assets that belong to me. I created them. Their entire purpose is to serve me…"

"You are trespassing on my property. I suggest you leave right this minute!"

"Or else what?… Mr Appledorn… Must we really let things get… ugly?"

We could hear something metallic clicking. I knew that click, I heard the same that night Thelma chased us with her shot gun.

"You get away from my house!"

A single shot echoed through the house. We could hear a body hitting the ground. Rose yelped and cried uncontrollably. Spirit was crying, gripping my hand.

Steps echoed through the house. Heeled shoes. It was her. She was coming. We could hear her stopping at the study and walking around it. She was searching for us. Then she entered the spare bedroom which we were not using. Soon enough she was at the main bedroom. She walked in. The door to the wardrobe opened with a bang. There she was, calm and unmoved, a gun in her hand.

"Hello One One Five Seven Two. I told you I would find you… you and your little friend who managed to fly under the radar for so long! Sneaky little bugger. Did you really think you could run away from me?" She chuckled. She was enjoying this little display of power. "You are MY property. Who do you think made you? *I* made you!" she was yelling. "I say it's time we ended the little 'happy family with mommy and daddy' charade, don't you?"

She pointed the gun directly at Rose.

Rose was crying, begging. I closed my eyes.

A single gunshot was fired. I shuddered. It was so loud; my ears were ringing. And more than that, my heart was breaking. I could actually feel it breaking – little pieces of it scattered inside me.

I opened my eyes.

The White Suit woman was standing there. Her gun was still in her hand, but her hand was now at her side. Not pointing. She had a wild look in her eyes… what was it? Bewilderment. A red circle was forming on her chest, getting wider and wider, soaking into the whiteness of her suit. She made a small sound. Her gun dropped to the floor, and then she fell. Her body crashed to the tiles in a heap, revealing behind her someone else standing, clad in black, holding a gun that was still smoking. The figure's top had an image of a person holding large pliers cutting into wires. The logo said *Dairy Slaves Liberation Front*, and underneath it, *Until all Farms Are Empty*. The shooter stepped over the White Suit woman and took her gun. Then the shooter came to face us in the closet. I could tell it was a woman. She leaned towards us and took the black balaclava off her face.

"Hi Sunny!"

I was not prepared. My mind was still whirling. I knew the voice. I knew those eyes. Big and brown. That big, beautiful smile. That mesmerizingly beautiful dark skin...

Pearl.

42 JONATHAN

"Pearl?"

"Yes"

"But... but... you were taken!"

"I wasn't taken, Sunny. I was rescued!"

I was still searching for some words, for clarity, waiting for my mind to reach some stability, when Rose jumped up.

Jonathan.

We ran to the front door. More of the black clad people were in the house now. Jonathan was lying on the floor. Surprisingly, he was not laying in a pool of blood.

Rose skidded to him.

"Jonathan! Oh no! No! No! Jonathan! Oh no! Please!... Please!"

A black-clad woman leaned towards Jonathan. She had long, shiny brown hair, held into a tail. She took his pulse.

"Rose, he still has a pulse!"

It was like an electricity bolt to Rose. She was a nurse, after all. She became all business after that, searching for the pulse herself, leaning to check his breathing.

"He's still breathing!" she said. Spirit and I gasped. "Violet, help me search for the gunshot wound"

Rose unzipped Jonathan's fleece jacket. The brown-haired woman helped her to remove it.

Rose started to unbutton Jonathan's shirt when she gently put her hand on his chest. Something in her face changed. I thought I might have even detected a teeny tiny smile. Her fingers were working now at double the speed to unbutton him. Underneath the shirt was a white singlet. Rose pushed her hand underneath the singlet. She was touching something. She was holding something.

Her hand came out from underneath Jonathan's white singlet. It was not covered in blood, it was holding something.

Something solid. Thick and golden.

Arabella's photograph.

43 DASLIF

"Why Jonathan, you sneaky bastard!" Violet exclaimed in astonishment.

Jonathan groaned loudly, a long, tortured groan.

"He was shot from a rather close range, he's still knocked out pretty badly," Rose said. "He is not quite out of the woods just yet."

"I'm sure you will nurse him well, Rose," Violet said, smiling at her sister.

Jonathan opened his eyes. Still groaning. He was very pale.

"Take it easy, love," Rose whispered to him.

"That was quite heroic," Violet said. She sounded quite amused. Her voice was not as warm and smooth as her sister's. It was somewhat deeper and more rustic.

Jonathan was coming around. Spirit and I allowed ourselves to kneel next to Jonathan. Spirit was closer. She took his hand and held it, still weeping.

"Hello little one," he said to her, smiling. "I'll be OK." His voice was weak and strained.

His eyes fell on me. Bright blue and kind. And there was something else… something deep. Gratitude.

Pearl put her arm around me.

Everything was more than a bit overwhelming. I was running out of breath.

"Let me fix everyone something cold to drink," Violet said. "Do you have some vodka?"

It took a while for the commotion to subside. Violet, Rose and some DaSLiF activists helped Rose take Jonathan to bed where she could nurse him back to health. He was badly bruised and had cracked a rib, but had no apparent internal bleeding.

Violet fixed everyone something cold to drink. I don't think it was vodka, but it did calm us down.

The activists, all clad in black, took the limp body of the White Suit woman and put her in the boot of her white car. I followed them outside.

"Is she dead?" I wondered, surprised at the knot in my stomach. There was too much pain and too much death around me already. I didn't feel like gloating at the fall of my enemy.

"No," Violet said, matter-of-factly, "but she is badly wounded. We have some facilities, not too far away, where we can take her and the other guy," she indicated casually at the white car. "There's quite a lot of invaluable information we can get from someone like her. Might even be able to rehabilitate her, eh? What do you think? Can you see that one as a DaSLiF activist?" She chuckled. I couldn't tell if she was being serious or not.

"We'll take care of everything, Rose," She said to her sister, suddenly with earnest. "Don't worry."

Rose, still very troubled, went back inside the house.

Another White Suit was in the car, gagged. They moved his bleeding body to the boot as well, wriggling in protest.

"You know where to take them," Violet said.

In no time the white car was gone, followed by a black car.

Suddenly, to my complete surprise, Violet put her arms around me, and gave me a big hug. I could smell her hair, flowery scented. She did not seem worried at all, not even a tiny bit shaken by all this.

"Sunny!" She said softly, "It is such a pleasure! Sorry I didn't introduce myself earlier, it's a bit chaotic here, as you can see." She smiled. She was quite a strong woman. She let go of me, still grabbing my arms with her hands. "Did you get a chance to see Pearl?" she laughed.

I was still searching for words. Searching for my brains.

"You know, that time we busted into your farm, we actually were aiming to rescue you! Would you believe it?"

I didn't know what to say. My mouth was open, but I still hadn't quite managed to dress all the question marks in my head with the right words.

"Don't be so surprised. We were watching you for a long time. But that night Pearl was one of the lucky ones, isn't it right, Pearl?"

"Yes Boss," Peal replied, giggling.

"She's all right, that girl," Violet said chuckling. "Though, she does need to work on her aim!" There was a playful, yet serious, tone to her speech.

Pearl seemed to be genuinely embarrassed. He cheeks darkened. "Sorry Boss," she said, then rapidly added, "I didn't panic, I was just in a hurry to save Sunny!"

Violet stroked Pearl's back fondly. There was a real sense of endearment in that moment. It confused me even more.

"So, the raid on the Farm... that was you? DaSLiF?" I asked, bewildered.

"Of course, who else?" Violet said, sounding almost bemused.

An activist who'd just finished cleaning up the mess in the house came out towards us.

Clad in black, his ash blonde hair cut short, a shock of hair was tossed casually to the side of his forehead. It was the first time I'd actually seen a young man up close. He must have been around seventeen or eighteen. He was smiling. His smile was warm and disarming. There was something about him... I don't know... I felt my heartbeat quickening a little. I remembered the way my mom had talked about the good-looking man. Back then, by that bush, I had no idea how to tell a man was good-looking. They all seemed the same to me. And there was the way Mom was looking at that man, that swaying of the thighs that I did not understand at all back then, but when the activist came to us I suddenly felt myself playing with my hair a little foolishly and flattering with my eyes more than necessary. I had no idea what was going on with me.

"Hi Sunny!" he said to me and reached out his hand.

"Hi," I said, my voice meek and girlie. I wanted to slap my own cheek with disgust at my odd behavior, but I just couldn't help myself. I shook his hand, melting a little.

"This is Ben," Violet introduced him. "One of the biggest brains and a definite future star of DaSLiF, but don't say it to his face, he might get a big head."

He chuckled. "Whatever you say, Boss."

"Ben was following you for a long time, Sunny," Violet said, amused.

"Violet!" Ben was protesting.

"You wouldn't guess what his nickname is…"

"Violet!"

"Sunny's boyfriend," she was laughing now. A real hearty laugh.

Ben smiled shyly… I smiled. I don't know why, it felt so weird, and kind of… flattering.

Time passed. To a bystander, knowing nothing of the occurrences of the past several days, it could all have seemed to be perfectly casual. we were just standing outside, socializing, chatting, making small jokes, catching up on lost time. As if the world around us was not completely crazy. My head was buzzing. I may have participated in the sociable chit chat, but I could hardly feel my own body.

After what seemed like forever, but was probably rather quick, the black car returned.

A young man and a young woman both clad in black came out.

"All done," the young man said. "The freaky woman is already in surgery. Alec said she has a 50-50 chance. He says Hi, by the way." Violet smiled a small, distracted smile.

"What about the other one, the White Suit man?" I wondered.

"The dude will live," the black-cladded young man said, nonchalantly. Then looking back at Violet, he added, "we got rid of the white car."

"Good job Nathan," Violet said, patting his shoulder.

"Do you shoot a lot of White Suits?" I asked, still feeling my head swirl.

Violet smiled a knowing smile. "We don't enjoy that part," she said. "But sometimes there is no other way. We have to do it."

I couldn't think of anything to say.

"Those you call White Suits will not hesitate before killing everyone around you and taking you back to the farm. But we only aim to disarm, or wound, never kill." She softened her voice, then added, "Believe it or not, we are actually *against* violence. We want to end it."

Rose stepped outside, quite disheveled, her hair a mess, streaks of tears marking her face.

"How is he?" Violet asked.

"He'll be all right... thank Mercy," Rose said, her voice tired. "It's time we had a good talk about everything," she said.

"Quite," Violet agreed.

"Let's get inside."

44 THE DECISION

Everyone except Jonathan sat around the coffee table in the living room.

"We knew that they were sniffing close," Violet said. "Somehow they were tipped off about you being in the area. We are not sure by whom or where they have seen you. But on that same morning they received a second call from someone at the village claiming to have seen you right there. The caller even gave a partial plate number, couldn't quite remember the rest," Violet rolled her eyes. "It was dumb luck, Rose. Not remembering the entire plate number certainly slowed them down." She sighed. "I told you, you took an unnecessary risk going there."

Rose nodded.

"Oh well, all water under the bridge now eh," Violet said. "Anyway, once they had a range, finding the house was easy enough."

"How do you actually know all this?" I wondered.

Violet smiled. "You would be surprised at what we can do, Sunny."

I don't know why, but I felt compelled to look at Ben. He smiled. My cheeks burned.

"I was meant to come here and meet Sunny, but we got some highly reliable intel that Jacqueline Roth was on her way, so I came with reinforcements."

"Is that woman, Roth – the White Suit?" Spirit asked.

"Natures' Bitch from Hell," Pearl said.

Well, I suppose she'd picked up a few new words in the outside world.

"Jacqueline Roth was the head scientist and one of the largest shareholders in Natures," Violet said. "She is not your problem anymore." She drew a deep breath. "But others will replace her. Until the industry is shut down, dairy slaves like you, girls and women, will still be used and bred and milked and killed."

Spirit winced.

"We have the house surveillanced, Rose," Violet said. "We've put you under 24-hour protection. You should be safe now." She turned her head to me, "Sunny, may I have a word please? In private?"

I nodded.

We walked outside to the deck and closed the sliding doors behind us. The sea was still playing its usual game of catch, completely unaware of the drama that just unfolded at its shore.

"Sunny," she began, but I interrupted her. Finally, my words were back and my tongue unstuck.

"You say that you were watching me for a long time... how? Why?"

"The data chip you had in your wrist before Rose and Jonathan took it out, that was how Natures farmers were tracking you. They got all of the information they needed beamed out to them, right out of your own hand. They could tell where you were, but more than that, that chip was so smart, they knew everything about you, what your body temperature was, when you ate, what you ate, when you shat, when your bleeding started... Everything."

I looked at my hand. Two faint stitches were still there.

"But we used the same technology to get that data too. And with time we even developed a data blocker. We would get the blocker in the air and interrupt their reception, that way we protected you from being 'read' but we could still receive your info. We even installed some models with cameras."

"The data blockers... do you mean... were these ... Sky Noise?"

"Black thing, flying in the sky... yes I suppose it was a bit noisy."

"That was you..."

"We noticed you a long time ago, Sunny. Your walks to the pond in the field, all alone. There was bravery about you that we don't often see in others. The attempt to break into The Shed at night with your friend…" Her face darkened then. "I am sorry for Rosy Cheeks," she said.

I nodded. Tears came to my eyes then. "She was just as brave as me, no less. And Spirit too."

"Undoubtedly. But there is another quality in you, Sunny. People follow you. You are a natural leader, just like your mother. Not everyone has that quality in them. It is a gift." She put her hand on my shoulder and gave it a squeeze. "Over generations, dairy slaves like you were artificially bred, refined over and over to create a subservient, obedient, docile, and fearful specimen that would not have the instinct to resist, that could bear children at an exceedingly younger age and produce the maximum amount of breast milk. But something happened, we believe, in the past twenty or thirty years or thereabouts…" She breathed in the sea air and let go of a deep sigh. "You give people power over creation and their egos get so overblown, they actually believe they are the creators, sweet Mercy"… she rolled her eyes. "We believe that at least one if not more of those Natures scientists started mixing their own sperm with the refined sperm… I don't know what sort of kick it gave them, to sire dairy slaves of their own genetic pool… It is rather messed up, the whole thing… But by doing that, they have in fact reintroduced resistance, independent thinking, criticism and courage into the breed."

Tears were rolling down my cheeks.

"It is quite possible that the change started with your mother," Violet added softly. She paused for a while, drawing another deep breath. "There is another thing you ought to know, Sunny."

"I know," I said.

Violet looked at me, wondering

"I know what you are about to say…" I wept, wiping my tears off my face, but they just kept coming. "I know that my mom is dead."

Violet nodded. "I am so sorry. How did you know?"

I just did. It was the way she kept coming to me in my dreams. She was still watching over me.

"Did they kill her?" I asked.

Violet nodded. "We traced her data to the end. She was shot. I am so sorry Sunny. We couldn't rescue her. We tried, but she refused to leave."

"What do you mean, you tried?"

Violet shuffled her feet a little. She cast her eyes to the sea, biting her lips as if she was contemplating something.

"OK, what I am about to tell you is top secret. You will need to keep this information to yourself. Under no circumstances should you share this with others. Lives might be on the line, do you understand?"

I nodded.

"We had an undercover agent who had free access to the farm. David. His cover was construction. He was often going in, fixing fences, gates, even toilet seats, you name it. He was DaSLiF but they had no idea. No one knew… except… he fell in love with Stella"…

"The good-looking man!" I blurted out.

"Yes, I suppose he was quite the looker, yes. It wasn't planned for him to get close to any of the dairy slaves but… oh well… I don't know many men who would be able to ignore your mother… She was such a stunning beauty… not much unlike yourself, mind you," she said and smiled.

"They had… a… relationship?" I asked.

"Yes. And it started long before the raid, Sunny. He wanted to reveal to your mother that a rescue plan was being devised. You and Stella were both supposed to be included in the rescue. But we forced him to keep his mouth shut. We could not have risked the plan being revealed and thwarted. In the end, you both escaped from the dormitories into the fields and we could not have risked our activists' lives by sending them after you. We rescued those who stayed behind in the buildings. Pearl was one of the lucky ones."

"And then?"

"We were planning another rescue but Stella begged David to wait. She was planning your escape and was afraid another raid would make security around the camp even tighter. She insisted we wait until after you were out... You should know that there were plenty of other opportunities for her to sneak out with David and leave the farm for good, but she always refused. She would not leave you behind, Sunny. Not you and not Antim. She loved you very much."

I couldn't stop crying...

"Was Antim... David's?" I had to ask.

"It is possible... maybe even likely, I don't know..." Violet said. "This is a secret that will forever be kept with them." She smiled a sad smile. "Stella told David that she was naming the baby Antim before the girl was born. It means 'final' in some language, she read it in a book somewhere. She was not going to let them breed her ever again, and that meant the end of her. She knew that."

"He was killed too," I said.

"Yes."

"Together with her."

"Yes. He came over to the farm after Stella burned down the women's dorms. We put up the data blocker to hide your whereabouts the entire time."

"Over the cornfield."

"Yes... But they already knew it was Stella's daughter who ran away from the breeding shed. David was trying to get Stella and Antim out. They were found out... someone snitched. There are always those in every farm..."

The dream I dreamed in that horrific night at Uncle Jessop's house came back to my memory very vividly. My mother and the good-looking man... David... holding hands and walking away from me. It must have happened that same day. The day we reached that house of horrors. My mom was telling me something in that dream. "Antim," she said, "Remember her..."

"Antim," I murmured.

"She is still in the farm, alive."

I wiped my tears. Violet handed me a tissue to wipe my nose.

She gave me a hug again.

"Sunny... I would like you to join DaSLiF," she said, and looked at me intently. "It is the reason I wanted to meet you for so long. You are courageous. You know that farm like the back of your hand."

"Pearl knows the farm," I said.

"Pearl was younger when she was rescued, she never wandered into the fields like you, and she was never inside the breeding shed. Plus, her memory of the place is fading... You can really help us bring it down. Think of all your friends who were left behind. Think of

Antim."

"What about Spirit?"

"She will be safe here with Rose and Jonathan," Violet said, "and you will be able to still be part of her life... of their lives... Bless my sister and her heart, she truly loves you both, you know?"

I smiled. I could sense the waterfall of tears was about to resume.

"Spirit cannot wish for a better family," Violet said. "And if at any point in time you would wish to resume your life here at the beach house nothing and no one would stand in your way... But I do believe there is a stronger calling for you Sunny... Will you join us?"

I knew this was a monumental decision that I was requested to make. I cast my eyes back into the room behind the glass doors. I looked at Rose and Spirit, sitting together, holding each other's hands. A pang of sorrow crossed my heart. That was my little family in there. Jonathan and Rose, they gave up so much for Spirit and me. They were so brave and so loving, and I loved them back. Right here, they provided me the home I wished for. After all we have endured... The constant fear... Rosichi giving up hope, the smell of her burnt body.... Uncle Jessop and the way he... he touched me... Then crazed Thelma Jessop and her shotgun... The White Suit woman breathing down my neck the whole time, reducing me to nothing more than a number... One One Five Seven Two... I closed my eyes. I would need to give up the beach house for a while... This house was the anchor I'd craved for, for so long, the beautiful hub of peace and serenity and love that I yearned for and needed... Do I just give it all up? For a life with DaSLiF? I opened my eyes and watched the activists, sitting together chatting, feeling very comfortable in each other's company. All wearing their black uniforms. Pearl, Nathan... Ben... A smile spread on my face again seeing him, darn it. I could fight alongside him... *'Sunny's Boyfriend'*... I liked that thought. I could help DaSLiF fight Natures farms. There was more than just *'my'* farm out there... there were many farms, and so much pain manufactured everywhere, and so much oblivion and indifference to it everywhere. There were more girls like me, like Rosichi and Dawn and Spirit and Antim... Antim. I could save her. I could help stop the pain before it happened. With DaSLiF, I could help the world to change. The world had to change. It had to.

I looked at the sea and drew the air deeply into my lungs.

I already knew my answer.

"Yes," I said and smiled to Violet. "I will."

Free your slaves. Go Vegan.

The end.

Made in the USA
Middletown, DE
20 September 2018